TATTOO

A
NOVEL

BY:

JACKIE McCONNELL

ESCAPE HATCH PRODUCTION MEDIA LLC

Printed in the United States of America for:

ESCAPE HATCH PRODUCTION MEDIA LLC

NOTICE

DEDICATION

I dedicate this and other works from my mind, body, and spirit to the Creator of all the worlds. For my continued knowledge of his existence has allowed me to prosper in all I desire.

ESCAPE HATCH PRODUCTION MEDIA LLC
CEO/JACKIE McCONNELL

WHAT ARE THE CHANCES?

THE GIFT

TATTOO

Tattoos are only superficial imprints of the irony that lies within.

Marks on the Soul

BOOK

ONE

1.

Poly-BioColor Incorporation is a huge conglomerate that supplies more than sixty percent of the dyes, inks, and paints the world consumes. Located in the high hills of Montana, the company known as PBC, flourishes on a hundred acre spread. A massive building built below ground is encased inside of a mountain. The landscaping around the facility display an entrance to an abandoned mine. Electrified fencing surrounds the entire perimeter. For the inquisitive passersby, a sign is posted to keep people safe. Access to the facility is through a special entrance.

One mile below surface, in a special ink pigmentation department, a government project is underway. Highly trained technicians worked miraculously on a phenomenal breakthrough, a discovery consistent with the use of neuron-pigmentation. The project is called iInk. For three years, the government poured unspecified amounts of taxpayers money into the project. The results were now bearing fruit.

***

Genesis Rodriguez entered a Manhattan tattoo parlor. She had been eyeing a particular piece of artwork for some time. Today, she mustered the courage to go through with it.

"Young lady, how may I help you?" asked the clerk. He was the proprietor of Urban Ink World, a new franchise that developed during the massive piercings and body art frenzy enveloping across the country. The parlor was brightly lit to display framed examples of artwork performed on premise. The rear held private booths for customers to relax while getting work done by highly professional personnel. The store owner, a middle-aged man, also wore multiple tattoos and piercings that were masterfully applied.

Genesis Rodriguez, a college student majoring in technical designs, saw a particular artwork that intrigued her enormously. It was an intricate pattern of intersecting lines. Genesis didn't understand why she was so attracted to it, only that she was. Her physique was perfect, lengthy black hair, well placed features, bone structure distinctive to people of European origin. Her family was from Spain. She was endowed with high cheekbones, rounded chin, almond shaped eye sockets, greenish-blue eyes, and a slender nose. Her appearance was appealing. She walked toward a walls that held framed designs.

"I like this one." Genesis pointed to a frame, and averted her attention to the owner.

"Excellent choice." Each design was done by a specific technician. The owner walked toward the wall and read initials placed under the framed design. It gave notice as to which technician was responsible for the artwork. "Are you ready now?"

Genesis took in a deep breath then released in the form of a sigh. She reluctantly nodded her head in affirmation. "Yes, I hope my boyfriend doesn't kill me for it."

"If you're ready please come this way." She was led to the rear of the parlor where numbered booths aligned the corridor. They stopped at a door marked number five.

The proprietor knocked before entering. "Rick, this lady wants number eighty seven." He adverted his attention to Genesis. "Please, take a seat." The two were left alone.

The technician, a tall man with slim features. He graduated from college as a graphic designer. In the beginning it was difficult for him to obtain employment in his chosen field. To support himself he accepted a job at Urban Ink World. The pay was great and the hours were flexible. He handed her a form. "Fill this out please."

"What is it?" Genesis gazed at the document.

"It's a release form giving authorization to have the work performed. If you want, I can even throw in a free design to go with the one you're getting." She signed the form. "Okay, let's get started. Please sit on the table." The procedure was underway.

2.

A dancer named Zesty entered Urban Ink World in Detroit,
Michigan. Her physical presence was captivating. Pleasant personality,
pretty face, and luscious body were charismatic. The employees at the
tattoo parlor were well-known in the community. Urban Ink World
was responsible for tattooing most of the dancers in the local clubs.

"Hey Chuck, I've decided to get another tattoo. This time I want
my stage name on my lower back." She pointed to her protruding
backside.

Chuck smiled. "Sounds great, it'll be my pleasure." He caught a
glimpse of her buttocks. "I'll tell you what, since you're a valued and
loyal customer, I'll throw in another design free of charge. How
about number eighty seven?"

"Okay, you've got yourself a deal."

Chuck handed her a form. "Fill out this form and I'll get
Johnathan. He's our best technician."

Tattoo

Chuck escorted Zesty to a private booth.

***

Five members from a high school varsity basketball team entered Urban Ink World. They were excited over their latest victory. The team defeated the rivals in a final elimination round. The group entered the shop with enthusiasm and excitement. The gathering attracted the attention from staff and customers.

A staff member approached. "How can I help you guys?"

The tallest of the group, the obvious center for the team, was the spokesman. The others headed for display cases with framed artwork along walls. The excitement took on different tones. "I would-I mean we would like to get tattoos that reflect us as a championship team."

"Okay, let's see what we can find." He escorted the young men toward the displays of artwork.

Four members of the group had already chosen their designs and were headed toward a sales associate. He wrote down their numbered choice noticing each wanted different designs. "How about if I throw in a quality design for all of you? It will show unity. Best of all, it won't cost you anything."

"That sounds great," answered the spokesperson. He was tall and slim with athletic features. His name is Rufus.

SIX

MONTHS

PRIOR

3.

POLY-BIO COLOR INCORPORATION
RESEARCH DEPARTMENT
GREAT FALLS, MONTANA

Lieutenant Satchel, a clean-cut man in his mid forties, and a prime subject in the armed forces. His chisel-like facial expression displayed no emotions, dark beady eyes exhibited a no-nonsense demeanor. Red blotches on his skin were reminders from his participation in the Desert Storm war. A land mine in Kuwait, laced with steel balls, was triggered in his vicinity by a first-tour of duty rookie soldier. The rookie died upon impact. Shrapnel reached the lieutenant, leaving hot metal fragments embedded in his skin. After recovery, Lieutenant Satchel was transferred and placed in charge of Urban Ink World, a testing pilot program owned and operated by the United States Department of Defense. Poly-Bio Color Incorporation spearheaded Urban Ink World as an outlet to reached numerous cities and citizens for research data. The lieutenant sat in front of a desk belonging to the president of Poly-Bio Color. Dr Theodore Benjamin held a prestigious degree in chemical engineering. Achievement plaques adorned a wall adding to the tasteful office decor. Every item in the room emphasized greatness. A large desk, leather chairs, antique lamps, and paintings gave the area an enriched setting.

"Yes lieutenant, data shows the experiment is a success. I think it's imperative we find human subjects to test it on."

Decretive metals aligned the breast pockets of Lieutenant Satchel's hunter-green uniform. A hat was ceremonially placed on his lap. "As you know doctor, we have a direct link to the public. Are you sure the preliminary test showed no adverse effects?"

Dr Benjamin nodded his head. "Yes, all of the tested laboratory specimens were a complete success." Dr Benjamin chuckled. "Inside the tattoo ink is a compound in which the molecular structure coincides with the genetic makeup of the nerve system. We are able to control the impulses sent to that system. Once introduced into the subject, we can alter their emotional range depending on the frequency setting. The government believes they can use this tactic overseas to achieve dominance."

"As far as I know, we're already deploying the ink in our government-owned franchise parlors called Urban Ink World," stated the lieutenant.

"That's great! All we have to do now is crunch the data and begin the coalescence."

4.

Genesis Rodriquez returned home early from work in hopes to surprise her live-in boyfriend Carlos Mendez. Carlos, a student at the same university, majored in computer science. The two shared a one-bedroom apartment in a ten-unit building. The dwelling was quiet and clean. What they both loved about the apartment was the fireplace in the living room. Crackling sound from rekindled logs filled the air, the ambiance was that of warmth and coziness. Halogen lamps were turned down low; a chilled bottle of champagne was submerged in an elegant stainless steel ice bucket. Genesis was ready. It wasn't long before Carlos entered the apartment. His senses picked up a lavender fragrance, and he followed the scent into a candle-lit bedroom. His eyes widened as he stared at his girlfriend on the bed. Genesis was propped on satin pillows that matched the color of the satin sheets. The sky-blue hue of the fabric glittered from illuminance emitted by candlelight. Genesis' pose was provocative and enticing. She wore an ivory colored negligee; the material silhouetted her curvy body. Her complexion radiated. Genesis sipped on champagne as she anticipated Carlos' return.

The sight and aroma tingled his senses. "Wow! What's the occasion?"

Genesis smiled. "Us, isn't that enough to celebrate?"

"Sure." Carlos approached the bed and kissed her lips.

"Why don't you go shower, and I'll keep things ready for you."

"Okay, keep that pose." Carlos hurried toward the bathroom. He stripped in transition, leaving a trail of discarded clothes in his wake.

Carlos exited the bathroom bare chested, a towel wrapped around his waist. Genesis patiently waited in the exact position he remembered. Carlos approached the bed and noticed a tattoo on her upper arm. The artwork depicted a flowery image with her name embedded into the design.

"When did you get that?"

"Today."

"Why didn't you tell me you were going to get it done?"

"Why should I have to tell you?" Genesis interjected.

Carlos felt an undercurrent of negative energy arise from the tone of the conversation. Although upset, he didn't want to argue. "I just thought we were in this relationship together. As partners, we should discuss major decision making."

"Major decision making?" Genesis felt indignation emerge from within. "First of all Carlos, there's no ring on my finger." She thrusted her hand forward to display a ringless digit. "We're shacking.

I don't think you really want the responsibilities of decision-making, as you say." She used her fingers to emphasize air quotes.

"I only meant I would have liked to have been there. Maybe I would have also gotten one."

Genesis smiled. "Just shut up and make love to me."

Carlos began caressing and kissing her. He was about to place Genesis in a submissive sexual position when he spotted another tattoo on the small of her lower back. The design was tasteful, but the artwork wasn't what angered him. "Genesis! What is this?"

Genesis turned to face him. "What?"

"The tattoo on your back…" He pointed toward it. "Why would you get something so intimately positioned without having a discussion about it?"

"Genesis studies his angered expression. "What? You don't like it?"

"No, it's not that. I think it's nice…" He hesitated in effort to find the right words.

"Then what is it?" She interjected.

"Honestly? The thought of someone touching you drives me crazy."

Genesis smiled. "You don't have to worry about that. I'm a one-man woman." She kissed him passionately. "I'll tell you what. How about you getting one just like this?" She pointed to the one on her lower back.

"Okay, for you I'll do it."

"Good, now make love to me."

5.

Zesty exited the Taste of Honey nightclub where she worked. Dressed in designer jeans and a silk blouse, she felt energetic and relaxed. Zesty carried a designer handbag that held her pay and tips. She attempted to placed her key in the vehicle door cylinder when a strong hand stopped her movement. She stared up at a man towering over her; his eyes were hidden behind dark eyewear.

"Stax!" she exclaimed. Zesty was startled by his sudden appearance. "I-I was just going to call you."

"Yeah? I'm here. What do you have for me?"

"I'm not doing well. The rent is late and I'm doing all I can."

"Tough shit! Do I look like I give a damn?" Stax snatched the handbag from her shoulders and rummaged through the contents, causing items to spilled onto the ground. He found what he sought after; an overstuffed envelope. Stax peered inside at the cash and smiled before pocketing the envelope. He handed her the handbag.

"I told you I need that! Don't I give you when I can? You're my protector, not my pimp. Please, don't get it confused. I'm not a prostitute." Zesty snatched her handbag from his grasp.

"Remember, you came to me when things were tough 'round here for you girls. Since then you haven't experienced any encounters with those crazy fools. You know why? I'll tell you. It's because I'm sponsoring you."

"I know that Stax. It was the reason why I came to you in the first place. We had a set price, now you're take advantage."

"Shut up! Do you know what I go through out here on these streets to keep you safe?"

"In that case your services are no longer needed. I'll take my chances on the streets alone," she retorted.

Stax was wide-eyed and taken aback by the outburst. He remembered his first encounter with Zesty, she was timid and afraid. "Okay, so you think you can handle things all by yourself?" He stared at her. "Okay, we shall see." Stax headed down the rain-slicked street as light drizzle covered the nocturnal setting.

Zesty stood near her vehicle as Stax headed down the darken street, she watched as he blended into the night and was out of sight. When the club closed, the area quickly became desolate. A cool eastern breeze gave her a frightful chill. Morbid thoughts entered her mind as she entered her vehicle and started the engine. Her trembling hands grasped the steering wheel, she drove feeling uneasy about the turn of events. Zesty lived across from a park in a sketchy section of town. The recreational area attracted troubled youths. During evening hours, it was not unusual to hear gunfire and police activity. At times she was kept awake all night from the calamity. Zesty entered her apartment building feeling exhausted. Rickety steps creaked as she ascended the stairs. No matter how gracefully she tried to tread, the noisier the steps became. She thought about the previous encounter, but felt too tired to give into any negative thought. She entered her apartment and flicked on a light switch. Normally, she would search for an alcoholic beverage to help with sleep; it wasn't necessary at the moment. After showering, she relaxed in bed and allowed sleep to win her over.

6.

After the encounter at Urban Ink World, the team of guys found their way to a neighborhood restaurant. It was one of the few places that remained open late. Most of the youths hung out enjoying the social experience, the atmosphere was relaxing and ecstatic. The best attractions were the food and inexpensive prices. The guys took a booth at the rear facing the main entrance. Popular songs played from obscured speakers inside the ceiling. Food and drinks were in abundance on tables. The group spoke loudly in effort to be heard over the din coming from other patrons seated around the room. Waiters and busboys moved about in efforts to keep up with the orders and available tables.

"You see that crew over there?" Dexter gestured with his eyes toward a table in the center of the room. Five attractive females sat eating and conversing. "They could be another gift for our winning streak." The guys viewed the girls.

"I know one thing. This tattoo is killing me," stated Stan.

"Man don't be such a baby. Man up! This is a brotherhood thing," retorted Chuck. Stan and Chuck were on the team the longest period of time, because the two were held back due to poor grades.

"Yeah! Those girls look nice but it's about us tonight," stated Damian, the quiet one in the group. "We've just become a brotherhood, let's toast." Cranberry juice-filled glasses clanged making a distinctive sounds. "To us, that we continue on life's path together and accomplish many great things."

***

The evening came to an end. Damian returned home where he lived with his mother and stepfather. He entered the house and headed toward the staircase leading to his room when a distinctive sound of someone clearing their throat erupted. Jolted by the sudden noise, he turned to see his stepfather sitting near a fireplace. The man was dressed in jeans, tee shirt, and boots. His stepfather's presence intimidated Damian, the man's beady eyes bore into his soul. He was tall, robust, mid fifties, and in excellent physical condition. Damian's biological father was killed at war in Afghanistan after the attack on the World Trade Center. He was six years old at the time. Later that year, his mother met Kenny Washington. They married eighteen month later. At first, Kenny displayed love and affection toward the young boy. Over time he'd began displaying dislike. Kenny secretly despised when his wife referred to her son as favoring his biological father more and more as time passed. Kenny felt as if he was competing with a dead man for her total love. His mother was unaware of the ill-emotion hidden in their relationship. She would leave Damian in his care while she worked, and Kenny would mistreat the child. Damian tried on may occasions to disclose his stepfather's behavior to his mother, but she failed to understand what he was revealing. She would dismiss it as exaggeration. Over the course of years, Damian grew mistrustful and withdrew from social activities until high school. At school he developed his basketball skills. The school's varsity team recruited him immediately after he displayed keen ball handling abilities.

"It's late and a school night," stated his stepfather. "Where have you been?" His gaze was stern.

"We won the finals against a rival school. The team and I went out to celebrate."

Kenny Washington stood; his tall stature overshadowed Damian. "That's not the rule in this house and you know it."

"I'm not a child anymore. You can't continue antagonizing me like you've been doing." Damian stood his ground and stared directly into Kenny's eyes.

His tone angered Kenny. "In that case you must be planning on getting your own place to stay."

"This is my father's house. You've no right to tell me to leave. If my mother don't have any objections, I'm staying."

"Oh really? We'll see about that." Kenny exited the room.

For the first time, Damian felt threatened by his stepfather. He was certain Kenny Washington kept a pistol in the house. Damian felt his life was in danger.

7.

Genesis and Carlos sat in a local diner not far from the apartment. Delightful foods filled the table. Burgers, fries, and salads were placed in front of them. The couple recently returned from Urban Ink World. Carlos had made good on his promise of getting an identical tattoo to the one Genesis received. He also added one to his liking on his arm. Carlos couldn't believe the pain associated with receiving a tattoo, he winced and rubbed his bandaged arm.

"I told you to stop rubbing it. You can cause it to get infected. You men don't have any threshold for pain."

Carlos sipped his beverage. "You know something Gen, I'll never understand what makes people get their entire body dipped in ink."

Genesis smiled with her mouth filled with food. She sipped ice tea to wash it down. "It's a fashion statement."

"After what I just experienced, I think it's pure craziness mixed with

S&M for pain freaks."

Genesis giggled, his expression amused her. "Let's eat and save dessert for later when we get back to the apartment." A seductive wink followed. Carlos smiled and nodded. Genesis sensed his uneasiness. "What's wrong? Don't tell me nothing. We've been together too long to hide our true emotions from one another."

I love her so much. "Honestly, I am worried about our tuition fees for this semester, and the bills at the apartment are beginning to pile up."

Genesis smiled and placed a hand on his cheek. "You worry too much. Don't we alway come out on top? Here…" She handed him her ice tea drink. "Drink some of this, we'll be fine."

Carlos couldn't bring himself to tell her about other arrangements he made to have the bills paid off. He realized there was no way she would approved of him doing any seedy dealings. Carlos' felt he was doing what was necessary for a man to take care of his woman.

The two slowly walked hand in hand after leaving the movie theater. The evening was delightful and the mood romantic. Carlos told one of his many jokes; the anecdote caused her merriment. As they neared a corner, Carlos saw a ball roll into busy traffic. Through his peripheral vision, he spotted a small boy dart after the ball. Focused only on the ball, the boy paid no attention to the oncoming dangers. Carlos viewed the scene in slow motion. The boy darted toward the center lane and used his foot to stop the ball's momentum. Horns blared from approaching vehicles. The boy was oblivious to his surroundings; he smiled and picked up the rubber ball. Carlos saw the oncoming traffic. The small child was not visible to the approaching drivers. His size, along with the evening hours, added to the dilemma. Without hesitation, Carlos darted after the child. He heard a loud shriek from the mother. Carlos reached the boy, picked him up, and darted toward the sidewalk from which he came. From that moment onward, reality became a blur. Vehicles approached at great speeds, horns sounded, and tires screeched as rubber fought for traction to stop. Carlos made a quick decision; he cleared the center lane and spotted Genesis' beautiful face. Her mouth was gaped from pure astonishment. Carlos tossed the child toward Genesis. A vehicle tried earnestly to come to a screeching halt, but the momentum was too great for the multi-ton vehicle to stop completely. Carlos was impacted, the force sent him airborne. He landed directly in front of a stationary school bus.

Everything seemed surreal to Genesis as motion slowed to a crawl. She envisioned the entire scene frame by frame as through the lens of a movie camera. Although she witness the entire incident, she wouldn't allow her mind to accept it as fact. The entire scene baffled her. One minute she was enjoying Carlos' company, the next moment she was catching an airborne child. A kid tossed by Carlos. Genesis heard the child's mother deafening cry for help. As the airborne child came into contact with her hands, Genesis grasped him tightly and secured him in her bosom. The short-lived feeling of triumph turned to despair when she witnessed a vehicle collide with Carlos. Genesis fell to the ground with the child resting atop. Her mind became overloaded with emotions as unconsciousness consumed her being.

Police and emergency vehicles appeared on the scene. A massive crowd gathered around the horrific site. Spectators were able to record the heroic act of Carlos with cellphones. In separate ambulances, Carlos and Genesis were taken to King's County Hospital.

Genesis remained in a self-induced coma, shock was the culprit of her ailment. She lay on a hospital bed while Carlos was taken to another area. Unbeknown to her, Carlos was pronounced dead upon arrival. The story went out on the internet like a wild brushfire. This was attributed by spectators with social media capabilities and police reports. At the time of the incident no identification was found on Carlos. Finding the next of kin was going to be a painstaking task. Luckily, the woman with him carried credentials. The information revealed she was a student at a local university. Police were dispatched to her home. At the time they didn't know the extent of their relationship. Using keys found on Genesis' possession, police officers converged on her apartment and entered the quarters. Their objective was to find any information on a next of kin. Inside the apartment they saw photographs of the two seemingly happy together. Upon further investigation in the apartment, they discovered items in a closet. The objects were located on the floor behind some boxes. The items recovered were cash and three kilos of high-grade heroin. The contraband was confiscated. Subsequently, police presence was stationed outside Genesis' hospital room waiting for consciousness to return; she would then be placed under arrest.

8.

The streets changed into strange shapes and objects Zesty could not comprehend. Directly in front of her eyes, the pavement reshaped itself. Symmetrical contours resembled steel rollers; ones used on conveyor systems. Breaking free from a strong hand grasped around her throat, Zesty found strength to run. She treaded urgently upon the difficult terrain noticing the rollers were moving at the exact speed of her own momentum. She sensed of running on a treadmill caused panic, her eyes displayed terror. She stared back at dark fingernails within reach; the hands belonged to Stax. His sinister gaze bore into the back of her neck as she continued to elude capture. Zesty heard obscenities shouted as she mustered strength to further the distance from his advances. Adrenaline rushed through her system resulting in increased heart rate. The drastic change in her metabolism triggered fear. A fork in the trail appeared. Zesty was unaware of her whereabouts, she quickly decided to head toward the right. Stax's warm breath was felt on the nape of her neck. *He's getting closer, what can I do?* She neared a bend in the trail; a loud ring tone permeated the space. The acute sound penetrated her ears and caused her eardrums to vibrate. Stax's hand gripped her neck…

Zesty awakened drenched in perspiration, her heart rate accelerated. The ringing sound of the telephone was prominent in the darken room. Closed curtains made it difficult for her to ascertain the time. She jumped out of bed and raced toward the sound. Groggily, she answered the call.

"Hel-lo?" Her tone was throaty as she spoke into the receiver. "Who is this? What time is it?"

"It's me Cheryl, and it's noon. Do you remember we have a hair salon appointment? You must have been hanging out all night."

"Nah girl, I've been having a terrible time. On top of everything, my sponsor…"

"Stax?" interjected Cheryl.

"Who else? He's been pressuring me to give him more."

"I thought you agreed to let him go. You know most of us girls did."

"I know and I did. He became belligerent and walked away threatening me. It kinda shook me."

"Don't worry, if he even thinks about…"

Zesty interjected. "Girl don't be silly." Her worrisome expression related her true feelings.

"What's wrong?" asked Cheryl. She sensed distress in Zesty's tone.

"I don't think I can make it. Stax stole my money when I refused to give him his fee. I don't even have enough to pay my rent let alone get my hair done."

"Zesty don't sweat it. I got your back. Com' over and we'll figure something out."

Zesty dressed and was about to leave the house to join Cheryl at the hairdresser when a knock came to the door. *Now what? It better not be Stax.* She sighed deeply and opened the door forcefully expecting to see Stax, she was fully prepared to explode. The sight of the landlord changed her entire demeanor.

"Mr Taylor, please come in. I was just on my way to see you."

"I hope it concerns the rent. You know you are delinquent. You are now living out your security deposit. I hope this isn't your way of saying you're leaving."

Zesty stepped aside to allow the landlord access. "I assure you that is not what is happening. I've been behind because I'm going through something. I know it's not your problem. I will have the money for you as soon as I return from work tonight."

The landlord was in his mid fifties and walked with a slight limp. The injury was sustained during active duty overseas. He wore a button-up shirt and slacks. Gray hair and facial lines added depth to his character. "Miss Crawford, if you don't have the money by then I will be forced to evict. You must know it will be a difficult task because you are one of the better tenants."

"I understand Mr Taylor." She escorted him out of the apartment. Zesty closed the door and sighed deeply to released pent up stress from within. Reopening the door, she headed out to meet with Cheryl. *I have a feeling it's going to be a long day.*

9.

The team ran drills with the air conditioner was out of service in the gymnasium. Coach Walker was a perfectionist; he pushed the boys to their limits to achieve his goal. The team respected his decisions because they were aware of his experience with the sport of basketball.

"Okay, that's enough for now. Make sure you guys take your salt tablets before going into the showers. Team you're doing great, keep up the good work." The guys filed out the area. "Damian, may I have a word with you?"

Damian was obviously exhausted. He stopped and headed toward the coach as sweat cascaded down his face. Perspiration dripped from his chin onto the highly polished parquet floor. "Yes coach, what is it?"

Coach Walker led Damian toward a bleacher seat. "I wanted to comment on the game. You seemed preoccupied in thought, you missed half the plays. Ones you yourself created and helped the team to master. I know when something is wrong. You know you can talk to me about anything. Everything will be kept confidential between us."

Damian gazed toward the floor as he contemplated his choices. He stared directly into the coach eyes. "It's nothing, I'm just fatigued is all."

Coach Walker sighed, he knew something was troubling Damian. "Okay, if you change your mind my doors are always open."

"Thank you sir." Damian jogged to catch up to the rest of the guys.

The guys walked the busy corridor heading toward their next class. "Damian what was that all about with you and the coach?" asked Chuck.

"He was just checking me about my game performance. I told him I just had an off day."

"Something is bothering you man. You botched up the three-one-two zone, and the pick and rolls. I know that ain't you."

"I ain't been sleeping right."

"What girl have you acting like that?" asked Stan. He held a firm grip onto his backpack as they headed through a crowded and noisy hallway. They were jostled by other students along the way.

"It's nothing." The guys began to separate and headed in different directions to their assigned classrooms. Stan and Damian remained together for science class.

The sounds of books rustling and chairs sliding on the floor were prominent in the classroom. Excited chatter hovered as the two sat adjacent to one another.

"You wanna tell me what's on your mind?" asked Stan. His brown eyes bore into Damian's eyes.

"If I tell you it has to remain between us."

"Sure." He scooted his chair closer.

"I think my stepdad is trying to hurt me, maybe even kill me."

"What?" Stan's voice raised. He regained his composure. "What makes you say that?"

"Last night we had some words. Really, it started long before that. Let me tell you…" Damian went on to explain his entire experience living with his stepfather. The teacher entered the classroom and demanded everyone's undivided attention.

"Class I want you to open your text book to page seventy nine." The teacher stood next to a blackboard at the head of the class. "Place all of your belongings in the desk, we're having a pop quiz."

Damian and Stan eyed one another; both were totally surprised.

10.

Fragments of light emitted through darkness, the spectrum intensified and spiraled out of control. Bright energy filled the void until darkness was no more. Genesis' closed eyelids fluttered from rapid eye movement, her blood pressure and heart rate elevated. Unfocused mental images replayed in the shadows of her mind; her eyes opened to an unfamiliar scene. She had no idea she was inside a secured hospital room. A white ceiling loomed overhead. Stiffness and pain set deep within her muscles and joints from prolonged immobility. Images of the past flashed across her mind's eye.

"Carlito!" she shouted. Genesis suddenly felt drained of energy; she tried to sit upright. Her restrained limbs baffled her as she heard the sound of metal chains rattled against the railing. "W-what's happening?" Her voice held a deep garbled tone; the symptom of dehydration had set in.

An officer sitting outside the door reading a newspaper heard the commotion and entered the room. His eyes widened as he witnessed Genesis struggle to breathe. He rushed out of he room and returned with a nurse.

The registered nurse hurried toward the patient to give aid. She addressed the officer. "Remove the restraints!"

"I'm sorry but..."

"But nothing! she interjected. "Remove them or her death will be on your hands!"

Having just three years on the force, the officer was trying earnestly to avoid any unnecessary demerits on his record. He thought about the ramifications if the girl died under his watch. He released the patient from the bed railing.

The nurse pushed a button on the bed. Genesis' head began to rise to an upright position. The nurse removed tubes from her nose and used a suction bulb to cleared all obstructions in the patient's nasal passageways. She placed an oxygen mask on Genesis' face and turned a knob on an oxygen tank. A hiss sound from escaped gas was audible. The officer observed the ongoings; he was confused as to what to do next. The nurse pressed the intercom button on the wall. A unified sound of her voice sounded throughout the hospital.

"Dr Baden. Room 119. Stat!" After making the announcement, the nurse took a pitcher of water from the table and half filled the glass. A doctor, along with two nursed, entered the room. The registered nurse referred to the officer. "Would you mind waiting outside?"

The officer looked toward the doctor who nodded approval. The officer turned around and exited without a word. All attention was now on Genesis. She was wide-eyed and seemingly confused.

"I called as soon as I noticed she was conscious. She was choking on her own fluids, so I sat her up and administered oxygen."

Dr Michael Baden, a resident physician, stood at five feet nine inches tall with salt and pepper facial hair. He wore a white laboratory coat over lime-green scrubs and a stethoscope draped around his neck. "You've done well." He turned to the other nurse. "Give me a reading on her vitals and some gauzes." He focused his attention on another nurse. "See if you can find any medical history files on her." The nurses went to do his beck and calling. He referred to the registered nurse. "You have other patients on this floor I'm sure. You are relieved to tend to your duties."

"Yes doctor."

He watched her exit the room. Dr Baden approached the bed and removed the oxygen mask from Genesis' face. He studied the chart at the foot of the bed. "What seems to be the problem young lady?" Genesis stared into his deep-blue eyes without answering the question.

"Blood pressure reading is one fifty over ninety five. Oxygen levels is regular. Heart rate is normal," stated a nurse.

"Okay, let's get you fixed up." His attention was on the nurse. "Get me thirty cc's of thiazide diuretic."

"Yes, doctor." The nurse exited the room.

"Waa-ter. Wa-ter," mumbled Genesis. Her voice was faint and dry.

Dr Baden studied the patient as he tried to make out what she meant. It dawned on him. "Thirsty huh? You want water?" He saw a glass on the table and placed it to her parched lips. Slowly he fed her water.

Genesis drank hungrily. The cool liquid was soothing. The oxygen in the water entered into her bloodstream, lowered her blood pressure, and relieved the lightheadedness she experienced. Genesis gazed at the room with no recollection of her whereabouts. "Carlos! Where is he? Why am I here?"

Dr Baden held up his hand. "Miss Rodriguez everything will be explained to you in due time. You are in a hospital. You've had a rough ordeal and collapsed. There are many accounts saying that you are a heroine. You saved a child's life."

"Carlos saved him! He darted after the child and tossed him to me. Then he was…" she succumbed to her emotions as recognition of the ordeal resurfaced.

"Let's get you better and then we can deal with the rest of the stuff later." After hearing about the incident that landed Genesis in the hospital, the doctor began feeling empathy for her. She didn't seem like a bad person. He believed there was a logical explanation for the police presence. A nurse entered with medication in a syringe. She passed it to the doctor. "Miss Rodriguez, I am going to send this medication through the intravenous tube in your arm to lower your blood pressure. You may feel yucky for a moment, but don't fret, it will pass. You will feel an intense urge to urinate. That is the result we're seeking." He administered the drug.

"Doctor when can I see Carlos?"

"He's in another section of the hospital. A staff member will soon come to visit with you."

"Will you please make sure he's okay?"

Dr Baden exited the room to see the officer standing in front of the door.

"Doctor my orders are to arrest her upon consciousness."

"That's not a good idea at the moment. She's experiencing a psychological ordeal. That bit of information could send her in the wrong direction." The doctor shook his head. "I forbid it."

The officer eyed the doctor. "How long will she be admitted?"

"I'll say one more day. Then she'll be in the safe zone and you can do what you have to."

"Okay doctor, I will notify my superiors. We'll have to continue security of the room."

"I understand." Dr Baden walked down the corridor on his way to find out about Carlos. *It's all I can do for her.*

11.

Lieutenant Satchel sat in a high-tech laboratory facing a computer generated global positioning system on a huge screen. Four technicians were seated along a complexed console adjusting dials. The screen displayed different locations across the country. The use of dot pixels revealed the locations of unsuspected carriers of the neuro-ink in the form of tattoos. The experiment was to cause the infected host to dispel violent behavioral eruptions. The experiment objective, if successful, was to be implemented overseas amongst the world's terrorist groups. The goal was to cause disruption from within the factions. The end results would lead to self-destruction. The scientist were in the early stages of development, a phase where live specimens were needed for testing. With the use of high security codes, the experiment was allowed to be tested on unsuspecting American citizens. It was carried out under a decree called National

Security Interest. The tactic wasn't new in concept. For decades, the United States used this style of research on its own citizens. In the early seventies, chemical agents such as Agent Orange were used in small portions on commuters in underground subway systems without any prior acknowledgment to the general public. In Japan, the same test was performed with documented deadly results.

"Dr Benjamin, how long do you think it will be before we will be able to give it a test drive?" asked Lieutenant Satchel. He was amazed at the technology. All across the country there were think tanks in use with the nation's brightest minds. If the test deemed successful, it meant an instant promotion for him. The thought caused him to smile.

"I would have to say another two days give or take." The doctor jotted data onto a pad from the screens as he talked. "Let me explain something to you so that you'll understand." He gestured with the use of a laser pointer. The device was directed toward a screen. "You see those lime colored dots all across the country? They represent our subjects in real time. When the full amount of the ink has been saturated into the host's organs, you will see the color of the dots turn dark green. That will notify us that the test subjects are one hundred percent under our control." He pressed a series of buttons and turned knobs on the console. Numbers appeared adjacent to the dots. "Those numbers represented the percentage of the neuro-pigments in their systems. As you can see it's a slow process."

"You need not worry, we have time." The lieutenant contemplated a thought. "I have one more question to ask."

"Fire away."

"To my understanding there were previous specimens of this nature. What ever happened to them?"

Dr Benjamin smiled, he was intrigued with the question. "There were two incidents that proved deadly, other than that it was effective. A postal worker in Arkansas went berserk and killed his fellow workers. Then there's a recent incident at a movie theater in Colorado."

"You mean to tell me those people weren't psychopaths? That they were influenced by your system to behave like that?"

"Yes. If you'll notice, all of them carried a tattoo somewhere on their bodies. Quite ingenious wouldn't you say?"

12.

Zesty was treated to a wonderful hairdo by Cheryl. It had the intended effect of changing her gloomy disposition to a softer side. Being with Cheryl was good because she was a true friend. After the visit with the hairdresser, they made their way to a quaint local restaurant for lunch. The two sat at a table near a window and sipped their favorite beverages while waiting for their orders to arrive. Zesty glanced out the window to admire passersby fashions. *Seems like everybody has somewhere to be.*

"Here…" Cheryl handed Zesty a wad of cash. "I know it's not nearly enough. Don't worry, we'll make something happen." Zesty studied the cash and felt self-conscious about asking for help. "Take it girl, or I'm going to be offended. I know you don't want me to be offended." Cheryl's expression was jovially sinister.

Zesty's uneasy mood swing was broken by Cheryl's facial gesture. She accepted. "I'll pay you back as soon as I can."

Cheryl's hand went up in protest. "Girl, you better not even go there." Cheryl's hairstyle was done in a close crop curl. Her slender nose, bronze complexion, and downward shaped eyes were attractive. "I also have a few things on eBay. I'll check to see if there are any purchases."

Zesty smiled. "Thank you." The food arrived; the dishes were delicious and delightful. Zesty's mind was partially on her personal situation and Cheryl sensed it.

"How 'bout that admirer you have at the club?"

"Who?"

"Don't you start. I'm talking about the old man that's always in your section everyday. He's the biggest tipper you have."

"And what are you saying?" retorted Zesty. "I'm suppose to sleep with him for money?"

Cheryl sipped her beverage and placed the glass on the table. "Don't act like you're some kind of saint." There was no response. "I didn't mean to say that." Cheryl snapped her fingers. "I have an idea! Let's get the girls together. I'm sure there's enough of us to make it work."

Zesty was reluctant. "I-I don't know." She didn't want her situation revealed to the others.

"Well I do!"

***

Eight ladies met at an eatery in a mall. Everyone greeted one another, they all carried the same complimentary tattoo from Urban Ink World. The ladies gladly pooled money together to help Zesty with her rent. It was a happy and heartfelt moment of solidarity.

Stax and a young group of guys sat in a vehicle on a quiet street located a block away from the club where Zesty danced. A total of four people were in the sedan. Two were seated in the rear; one in the front passenger seat next to Stax.

Stax referred to the guy in the seat adjacent to him. "Delroy, I'm giving you this cash to do what I asked. Don't touch her face, she has to work. Understand?"

Delroy eyed Stax with caution; his facial expression displayed bafflement. "Let me get this straight. You want us to rob Zesty? One of your girls? Whatever we take is ours, and you'll pay us to do it? I don't get it. What's the catch?"

Stax's smile exposed bejeweled teeth. "Let's just say I'm teaching her a lesson. Do you guys think you can handle it?"

"Yeah sure."

"Yeah."

"Sure thing." The guys looked to one another. Simultaneously, they exited the sedan leaving Stax in the vehicle.

Stax watched the guys headed toward the mark. Each wore black hooded sweatshirts, dark jeans, and black boots. He glanced at his wristwatch. *She should be about finished. When this is over, she'll beg to get me back.*

The Taste of Honey club was winding down. The evening was busy as usual. The place was trashed; liquor and beer bottles were strewn about. The dressing room was quiet, most of the dancers were gone for the evening. The sound of metal locker doors closing were pronounced in the confined space. Zesty and Cheryl were the only ones that remained, they were in preparation to leave.

"I really want to thank you Cheryl for having my back. You guys really mean the world to me. I will be there for all of you." Zesty's moistened eyes displayed endearment.

Cheryl retrieved her keys from the locker and closed the door. The sound reverberated. She approached Zesty. "I don't want you to feel you're in our debt. Remember, what is given from the heart stays with the heart." The two embraced.

"We're gonna be fine," encouraged Zesty.

They stood apart and gazed into one another's eyes. "Are you gonna be all right? Do you want me to wait on you?"

Zesty wiped her tear soaked eyes. "Nah, you go on ahead. I'm okay. I just have a few more things to get. I'll see you tomorrow."

"Sure thing."

***

Delroy and his boys waited out of sight. The only activity were stragglers exiting the club. Most headed toward their vehicles. Delroy watched from behind a vehicle as Cheryl entered her vehicle and drove away.

"Man she looks…"

"Cool it! We're not here for that," interjected Delroy. "Focus!"

They inched closer to the club on the darkened street. Delroy spotted Zesty's vehicle from the description Stax had given. The nocturnal skies suddenly parted allowing rain to descend on the streets. Surfaces became slick from an intense downpour.

"Damn! That's all I need for the rain to mess up my hair." Zesty wore a tan leather jacket and blue jeans. A designer clutch bag clung to her shoulder as her keyring dangled in her hand. *I've done pretty good tonight. I can't wait to get home and sleep.* She jumped across a puddle onto the street. Her outfit became soaked. Zesty's saturated hairdo clung to her skull. Using her clutch bag as an umbrella, she placed her key in the cylinder of her vehicle. A searing pain was felt in the back of her neck. The pressure was intense, the force caused her body to slam onto the side of the vehicle. Before she could regain her composure, Zesty felt her bag being snatched away. The downpour of rain distorted her vision. She felt disoriented and pained. Faintly, she could hear the sounds of footsteps splatter in the puddles as the intruders fled. Zesty gazed through the blinding rain at hooded figures. Rain drenched, she made her way inside the vehicle. Fear overwhelmed her emotion. She partially regained her composure before driving away. Agitated about the incident, Zesty drove aimlessly. The street signs and traffic lights became a blur. Her stomach was in excruciating pain as if someone had kicked her. The sound of the wiper blades scraped across the wet glass leaving smeared marks. She planned to have them replaced months ago, but never gotten around to doing it. Her vision was now obstructed. *Who were those guys?* Zesty gazed through the window and saw Cheryl's apartment building, she'd subconsciously drove there. Zesty knocked on Cheryl's apartment door and stood back as the peephole latch engaged. The door was answered by Cheryl dressed in a nightgown.

"Girl what happened?" Cheryl stared at Zesty's drenched clothing, disheveled appearance, and quickly pulled her into the apartment. "What happened?"

The sight and sound of having someone who genuinely cared was much to bare, the dams in the corner of her eyes gave away allowing tears to cascaded down her cheeks. "I-I was mugged by a group of boys outside the club."

"Oh my! Look at you! Come…" Cheryl escorted her toward the bathroom. "Take off those wet things. I have some dry clothes for you to put on while I wash and dry those. Are you hurt?"

"My stomach aches where one of them hit me, other than that I'm fine. I guess it's more my pride hurting than anything else. I realized how much I've dumped on you in the last twenty-fours."

"Nonsense! Get changed before you catch the death of cold. You want coffee?"

"Yeah, that would be nice."

The ladies sat in the kitchen drinking coffee. Zesty was dressed in comfortable lounge wear belonging to Cheryl, who refused to let her go home and be alone. Zesty explained the entire incident.

Cheryl became irate at the conclusion. "Those bastards! Who do they think they are? Why can't they find a job like everyone else?"

Zesty didn't respond, her mind recapped the entire event in hopes of making sense of it.

"What's wrong?" asked Cheryl. She sensed Zesty's ill feeling.

"I can't help thinking I was targeted."

"What do you mean?" Cheryl was intrigued.

"There were others leaving the club before me. Why me?" She shivered at the thought.

"If that's the case, who would do something like that?"

"Stax!"

"Stax!" It was said in unison.

13.

Damian had the guys over his house studying from a new playbook. They were in the basement while his mother and stepfather were out. The group were memorizing plays, and testing one another on their ability to recall.

"Remember, first you have to have it in here..." Stan pointed to his head. "Then, you execute it on the court."

The sound of footsteps adverted their attention. The door opened and Kenny Washington entered in the room. He observed the group's activities.

"I'm sorry boys, but you'll have to come back at another time. Damian has chores to do." He stared at Damian disdainfully.

The guys were startled by Damian's stepfather's presences and gathered their possessions. Damian stood at the other side of the room fuming with anger. He faced his stepfather.

"Why did you have to do that?"

Kenny Washington's stylish appearance included a button-up shirt and dark slacks. "Because I can! Don't you question my authority boy."

"I'm not a child anymore."

"Oh no?" retorted Kenny Washington. "Okay, the light bill needs paying. We need to replace the furnace over there. Which bill are you gonna help out with?" Damian remained silent. "I figured as much! Until you can afford to help out around here you're just a kid to me." A noise came from the top of the stairs. Damian's mother, Kenny's wife, returned from shopping. "We'll discuss this at another time." Kenny headed up the stairs.

"No! Not later. How about now?" Damian inched closer. His confidence soared knowing his mother had arrived. "Why are you so nasty to me? I've never done anything to you."

"Don't you take that tone with me. You know…" Clair descended the stairs.

"What are my two men up to in the basement?" Damian's mother was dressed smartly. For her age, she was shapely and an eye-catcher. Her complexion required no makeup; her scent was pleasant.

"Hey honey." Kenny kissed his wife.

"Hi mom." Damian followed suit. "We're just talking. I had the guys over going over plays."

"That's nice dear. Can you help me?

"Sure mom."

"The groceries upstairs need to be put away. Will you do that?"

"Sure." Damian gave Kenny a lingering stare before heading up the stairs.

She turned toward her husband. "What were you two up to?"

"Just bonding." He clasped his hand into hers and led the way upstairs. "Come on, I want to show you something."

Fuming over the incident, Damian continued to put away the groceries. His mind was in turmoil. *I'm tired of the way he treats me. I should kill him.* His thought was intercepted by rational thinking. *That would crush my mother's spirit. No, there has to be another way to keep him away from me.*

14.

Dr Micheal Baden entered the room unannounced, his sudden appearance startled Genesis. She sat up in bed and stared into his eyes in effort to read his demeanor, hoping to find out about Carlos' condition, but the doctor's facial expression was emotionless.

"What did you find out about Carlos? Where is he? Is he all right?"

Dr Baden approached the bed and placed a supportive hand on Genesis' shoulder. "I'm sorry to be the one to inform you. Carlos didn't survive, he died of a punctured lung caused by the impact of the vehicle. I'm sorry." He stood back feeling empathy for her loss.

Tears covered Genesis' face. Mixed emotions overwhelmed her senses. Her body trembled as she stared at the doctor. "How? Why? Carlos was a good man. Did you know he saved a child's life?"

Dr Baden nodded. "Yes, he is a true hero."

"I know he's in heaven." Uncontrollable emotions erupted. "I don't want to live anymore either."

"Nonsense! Don't say that, everything will work out. Something good will come. You'll just have to give it time."

"No! It will not be all right." She became grief-stricken.

Dr Baden exited the room onto a busy corridor where staff were being paged on a public address system, and employees moved about doing day to day duties. He motioned for a nurse to approach.

"I want Miss Rodriguez to have 250 milligrams of chlorpromazine prescribed now."

"In what form doctor?"

"Injection would be most effective. I want her sedated due to emotional distress. She's been through a rough ordeal."

"Yes doctor."

The nurse turned and walked away. The officer guarding Genesis stood and approached the doctor."

"Excuse me doctor. I was told to read her the Miranda rights as soon as she became conscious."

The doctor studied the officer. "That's impossible. She's incoherent at the moment and a mild sedative was just prescribed. I'm sorry, that will not be possible at this time."

"Large amounts of narcotics were found in an apartment leased to her. I don't know if it belonged to Miss Rodriguez or the deceased boyfriend. My superiors want action."

"If my understanding is correct the two saved a life. Is that not correct?"

"Yes it is. Doctor, all I am trying to do is my job."

The nurse approached with the subscribed drug in a syringe. The doctor adverted his attention to her momentarily and nodded before eyeing the officer. "You will not be able to exercise your mission at this time." Dr Baden followed the nurse into the room and closed the door.

Genesis was an emotional wreck, her once neatly combed hair was now in disarray. She squeezed the sheets tightly in her hand; her thoughts were elsewhere. Genesis was oblivious to the intrusion of her privacy.

Dr Baden approached the bed with the syringe in hand. The nurse used an alcohol pad on Genesis' right forearm before the doctor injected the sedative into her system. Genesis was overwhelmed with so much emotional turmoil, she didn't feel the prick of the needle as it penetrated her skin. The effects of the drug worked immediately and Genesis began to relax. Within minutes, sleep overrode her will to be conscience.

"I want her under constant surveillance. I also want vital readings performed on the hour."

"Yes doctor." The nurse watched as the doctor exited the room.

Dr Baden's mind was intrigued with curiosity. Usually, he wasn't affected by any of his patients on a personal level. This patient was different. Strangely, a deep-seated concern for Genesis' wellbeing existed. The officer outside the room caused the doctor to feel uneasy. He continued down the corridor without saying a word to the civil servant. *I'm sure there's more to this.*

Dr Baden entered his office, sat behind his desk, and picked up the telephone. The call was answered on the second ring. "Connie it's me, I need a favor. I have two names I would like ran through your database." He related the names to the recipient on the other end of the call. "Please, call me back on my cellphone when the information becomes available. Thank you." The line was disconnected. Dr Baden sat contemplating the scenario and his involvement. His eyes were diverted to photographs on his desk. They were of his grandchildren. He summarized the event with Genesis and concluded he would want someone to help his child if they were in troubled.

15.

The last staged act at the Taste Of Honey Club ended thirty minutes ago. The dressing room had emptied leaving, Zesty alone in the basement. Her act was the last performance, she could hear the cleaning crew upstairs vacuuming. Zesty wore form-fitted jeans, cotton blouse, and a waist-length jacket. She exited the building filled with apprehension; the prior incident left her feeling insecure. Glancing at her surroundings, and armed with a canister of mace, she stepped from the club onto the street. The velocity of the wind was low, but a chill entered her body. Zesty noticed a sedan moving slowly in her direction as she placed a key in the vehicle door cylinder. Nervous, she braced herself for trouble by holding firmly onto the mace in her right hand. The driver came into view. *Damn!* Zesty stood defiantly as Stax's vehicle came to a full stop adjacent to her.

Stax exited the sedan wearing dark slacks and a sweater. He

approached. "How are you doing?" Zesty remained silent. "I was in the neighborhood and spotted you. What's up?"

"Look Stax, cut the bullshit! What do you want? You and I know everything you do has a motive." Zesty positioned a hand on her hip as stared at him. Her gesture displayed a no-nonsense demeanor.

Stax smiled. "I heard you ran into a little trouble. I was wanting to see if you were okay. Do you need anything?"

"Yeah, there is something I need. How 'bout the money you took from me? I would like it back."

Stax smirked. "Okay, I deserved that."

"No, you didn't deserve that, I did. It was my money not yours."

"Okay, I see your point. Now that I see you're okay, I'll be on my way." Stax returned to his vehicle.

"If you came here to see if the goons you sent hurt me, the answer is no."

The statement caught Stax by surprise. He stopped and stared at her as he sat in his vehicle. His expression displayed displeasure. "What did you say?" His beady eyes gazed at her.

His demeanor summarized everything to Zesty. She knew she'd struck a vein; one that was dangerous. The thought of him stooping so low infuriated her; she went a step further. "That's right you heard me. I know about your little goons, and I think you're pathetic. I have no more respect for you." Zesty realized she was treading on thin ice. She sat in the vehicle with the doors locked and the engine idling. Stax exited the vehicle and approached Zesty. He gazed at her through the closed window. Zesty saw he was upset; spittle eject from his mouth as he spoke. The vehicle's tight seal made the audio of his voice impaired.

"I'll tell you something. I don't know where you've gotten your twisted little information. I see now why you were targeted, your mouth is too big." Anger overwhelmed him, he hit the driver side window with an open-palm hand.

Not wanting the situation to spiral out of control, Zesty placed the vehicle in gear, stepped on the accelerator while keeping her eyes partly on the rear view mirror. She saw that Stax was upset and continued to yell as she drove away. Zesty hurried toward the avenue, hoping the crowd of other vehicles would deter any ill motives on his part. Traffic at the early hour was nonexistent. She turned onto the expressway. *Wow! That was a close call.* Zesty continued driving on the expressway. After passing a few exits, she began to feel a sense of ease. Suddenly, a loud thud noise erupted and Zesty lost control of the vehicle. It began to spin. She glanced at her rear view mirror and realized what was happening. Zesty fought furiously to regain control of the vehicle. Seeing the sedan in the rear view mirror sent mixed emotions into her being, fear and anger dwelled simultaneously within. Zesty's vehicle hit a guard rail and continued down an embankment. The vehicle hit a spruce tree. The sudden impact caused the driver airbag to deployed; an explosive pneumatic shriek and material engulfed Zesty. The seat belt restrained her movement.

Stax drove next to the damaged vehicle, and glanced around the roadway to assure they were in seclusion before exiting. He glanced at his mud saturated shoes. "Dammit!" He approached the wrecked vehicle. Audible sounds of moans existed. "You see what you made me do?" He glanced at his vehicle then adverted his attention toward

Zesty. "You made me scratch my fender on this piece of shit." He gestured with his hands toward Zesty's wrecked vehicle.

Her voice was low and garbled. "G-gett me outta here." She was badly shaken.

"Oh now you need my help? Just before you were so brave and self-sufficient." He saw blood running from her nose, and that wedged between the airbag and the seat. The seat belt held her in place. He retrieved a switchblade from his pocket and punctured the inflated airbag; a mild hiss ensued following the airbag retraction. Stax reached over and released the seat restraint from around Zesty's chest and waist.

As soon as Zesty heard the release mechanism on the seat belt, she sprung into action. With the use of mace, she sprayed a direct stream of compressed gas into Stax's unsuspecting eyes; his scream was deafening.

"Aaahhh!" Agony engulfed his being. Stax held onto his face and rubbed his closed eyes. Zesty continued to spray until she emptied the entire content from the canister. His breathing became impaired, he fell back onto the dampen ground soiling his entire outfit. His shrieks continued.

Zesty stood over him. "It's no fun when the rabbit has the gun is it?" She felt no remorse; her next move was to tell Cheryl what had happened, and maybe call the police.

***

Impatient to find out the progress of the project, Lieutenant Satchel arrived at the laboratory after being notified more test subjects were in the green zone and ready for activation. He was excited to get a first glimpse at how the system was being implemented. Lieutenant Satchel was the only personnel adorned in military uniform. The entire staff of technicians wore lab coats with name tags and visible security clearance badges. The sounds of beeps and clatter from keyboard programming resonated in the sterile environment.

Lieutenant Satchel sat in a seat facing a massive digital monitor. Dark-green dots were positioned throughout a virtual map of the United States. Most of the subjects were in the mid-stage of completion.

"Okay, what do we have going on?" asked Lieutenant Satchel. His question was to a chief technician.

The technician, a man in his mid forties, took a seat next to the lieutenant. His hair was neatly trimmed, he wore spectacles on his aquiline nose. "You see that dot?" He motioned with a laser pointer. "The one in the area of central Detroit. It just came online as being ready for activation. Watch this…" The technician turned a series of dials on a control panel. The procedure was a mystery to Lieutenant Satchel, he eyed blinking lights, graphs, meters, dials, and switches. A huge monitor commanded his attention. "Okay, let's see what you've got," said the technician. He spoke to no one in particular. His attention adverted to the lieutenant. "In a moment the satellite communication feed will be triangulated to that sector. We will get a visual and audio feed from the location. At this moment we have no idea who these people are. That's for security purposes only. All we are required to obtain are the waivers signed by the subjects at the time of receiving their complementary tattoos."

The lieutenant was intrigued. "I still can't believe the Colorado theater shooter and the face-eating maniac were your test subjects.

"Truthfully, that's the part I find disconcerting. Especially when the subjects gets into trouble, they're on their own having no explanation for a motive. It allows the media to speculate and disperse fragmented truths onto the general public." The technician gazed at the lieutenant. "Lieutenant, you of all people know that without commitment and sacrifice there would be no United States of America as we know it today." The monitor displayed images on the screen in real time. Both men looked on intrigued.

***

Zesty walked away from Stax. Suddenly, a strange sensation overwhelmed her being; a bitter metallic taste saturated her mouth. Zesty's mind went blank, her thoughts were overridden by an unknown phenomena. She stared at a strange creature on the ground. There was no recollection of Stax's identity. Zesty sensed an out-of-body sensation. No longer in control of her action, she felt compelled do the will of an unknown force. Zesty picked up a large rock from the grassy marsh and held it overhead. Normally, she would have struggled with the weight and size of such an object. She brought the stone down hard on the head of the strange creature. The creature's movement stopped. Unattached, she slowly walked toward her vehicle in a trance-like state and retrieved the keys from the ignition. She headed toward the sedan idled on the side of the road, entered and drove away.

***

Lieutenant Satchel and the technician watched the subject on the huge monitor. After the ordeal, they studied one another's expression; both men displayed pure disbelief.

"I have to conclude it was a success," stated the technician. He typed data into the computer files.

"I guess you're right if we call cold-blooded murder a success."

"Just imagine. If this were an insurgent, it would have been scored as a home run."

16.

Damian sat with his teammates at a neighborhood recreation center, the setting was lively with local youths playing different arrays of table games. Classroom instruction was in progress to help kids with academic studies. Damian and the team sat in the bleacher section watching a basketball game in progress. The guys huddled together to avoid being overheard.

"How did it go with you and your stepdad?" asked Dexter.

Damian shrugged his shoulders. "I don't understand him, he's just mean to the core. He shuts me out when I try to confront him. When my mom enters the room, he tries to make like everything is cool. He makes me so angry."

Stan gave him a sympathetic pat on the shoulder. "Don't sweat it man. You're almost at the age of consent. Soon you'll be able to leave and go on your own."

"I don't think I can leave him in that house alone with my mother."

"What do you mean?" asked Dexter.

"I don't have any proof, but I think he's doing something to her."

"Like what?" asked Rufus.

"I don't know exactly. It's not physical abuse or anything. Otherwise, I would have been all over his ass. She must sense the undercurrent between him and I."

"Maybe there's more to it you just don't know about." Chuck palmed a basketball in his left hand.

Damian faced him. "Such as?"

Chuck shrugged. "I don't know. Ya'll wanna go challenge those guys over there?"

"That sounds like a plan. Let's go." Stan led the way; he was happy the subject changed.

The guys joined a group on the basketball court for a game. Spectators stopped activities to watch the matchup. From the start of the game, the intensity quickly heightened. Damian was surprised to discover the opponent's skill levels were impeccable. The third quarter turned into a trash-talking session from both sides. Physical contact became prominent as excited spectators cheered on.

***

Lieutenant Satchel continued to view the monitor; he gazed the dots plastered on the screen. The images reminded him of a marketing billboard. He anticipated the praises he would received from his superiors. "How about the dots on the left?"

"Those are in the stage of completion. Let's see what we have." The technician turned a few dials on a panel. The graphics revealed five test subjects in the same locale. "It could mean the doses were administered simultaneously." He pressed a few control buttons, and the graphics focused on an aerial view of a building. Touching more control switches allowed the satellite to connect directly through the structure. A crowded area of youngsters came into view on the monitor. Subjects playing a game of basketball zoomed in. "That's interesting." The technician flipped a switch. "Let's see what happens when we activate the ink in their nerve centers."

***

Stan fell forcefully on the hardwood floor in an attempt to save a ball after Dexter's shot attempt failed. He was pushed by his opponent and angered by the play. Suddenly, his body temperature elevated from within. A strange sensation enveloped his body as a metallic taste filled his mouth and leaving a bitter aftertaste. He closed his eyes for a moment to internalized what was happening. Stan opened his eyes to see his opponent's eyes were flaming red; they leered at him as fear took hold. Suddenly, he was no longer in control of his being. Stan quickly stood as the unknown entity neared. The creature pointed what seemed to be a talon-like finger. Stan gazed at his friends. They too witnessed the same phenomena. Without hesitation, the five-man group sprung into action. Their opponents were confronted and subdued skillfully. Each were held in lethal choke holds by Damian and his teammates. As if rehearsed, each man simultaneously struck, killing their opponents instantly.

Spectators were ill-prepared for the turn of events. Fearful for their own safety, they rushed frantically toward the exits. Chaos exploded as people were trampled in effort to escape. Staff moved methodically trying to regain control and gather information as to what was taking place.

Damian and his group suddenly regained control of their being, and gazed at one another bewildered. Panic-stricken, they rushed toward the exit.

***

"I don't believe it! Technology and power to make things like this happen would be devastating if it were to get into the wrong hands!" The lieutenant awaited a reply.

"There you have it. Project i-Ink is a success. You can call it in."

"No, not just yet. I want to see more before we call in the cavalry."

"Suit yourself."

17.

KING'S COUNTY MEDICAL CENTER/
SECURED OBSERVATION WARD
BROOKLYN, NEW YORK

Genesis Rodriguez's eyes widened when Dr Baden entered the private quarters. He was notified the moment Genesis became conscious. After making an inquiry about the history of Carlos, Dr Baden came to the conclusion she was being framed. He'd witnessed similar situations in the past and was aware how unsuspected victims were used as pawns to carry heavy burdens under the law. The doctor wore a laboratory coat with a stethoscope draped over his shoulder. He removed a chart board from the side of the bed and glanced at the information before staring at Genesis.

"How are you feeling Miss Rodriguez?"

Genesis gazed the doctor without giving a response, her greenish-blue eyes were overshadowed by red blood vessels. The lost of Carlos was devastating. *Why wasn't I nice to him?* She gripped her disheveled hair as grief took hold.

Feeling empathy, Dr Baden touched her shoulder. "Get it all out. A good cry cleanses the soul." After the emotional outbreak, Dr Baden studied her pupils using a light to scan her orbs. The doctor realized the red veins were an indication Genesis' blood pressure was elevated due to her grief-stricken condition. During his practice, the doctor learned symptoms as such can cause elevated heart rate. "Miss Rodriquez, I'm not going to sugarcoat things. You are in a secured section of King's County Hospital. Meaning, police are outside the door waiting the opportunity to read Miranda rights and arrest you. Can you remember anything prior to coming here?"

Genesis studied the doctor's demeanor and sensed pure concern. She wiped tears from her cheeks with the back of her hand. "Carlos and I were walking and a child darted into the streets after a ball. It all happened so fast, I remember the child being airborne." Genesis placed her hands to her face as she recalled the dreadful memory plastered in her brain.

"Okay, this is what I've gathered from your ordeal with a little research of my own. Carlos didn't have any type of identification on his person at the time of the accident. Your personal effects included school identification and home address. In efforts to locate the next of kin, they went to your apartment. While on the premises, they discovered photographs depicting the two of you shared the same dwelling. Further investigation led them to the conclusion you were both students at the same university. You were both struggling to pay your tuition on time each semester. The clincher is what was found in a closet space. They were looking for identification when drugs and cash were discovered. You were brought here." Dr Baden noticed she displayed genuine bewilderment. "My feeling to all of this is you didn't know anything about it. Carlos is deceased, so he can't defend himself. That leaves the authorities blaming you."

"B-but how can that be? Carlos isn't a drug dealer. As you said earlier, we were struggling students. Oh God! What am I going to do?"

"Don't you worry. As long as you're in my care, they cannot touch you. The only problem, I don't know how long I can justify postponing the inevitable."

"Why are you helping me?" Genesis stared into the doctor's eyes.

"Let's just say I don't like when injustice is being committed. Especially, to a heroine." He gestured with a wink.

The statement produced a smile from Genesis. "Thank you doctor."

"You're quite welcome Miss Rodriquez."

"Please, call me Genesis."

"Genesis it is. Your name in the Hebrew language mean the beginning. The first thing I'll need to record is your bloodwork. Roll up your sleeve young lady." He walked to a locked medical cabinet and retrieved a syringe along with other paraphernalia used to extract blood. "This will buy time until we can figure what the next move will be." He exited the room carrying several vials of Genesis' blood. Preoccupied in thought, the doctor didn't realize the officer outside the door studied his movement.

The officer placed a magazine he browsed on an adjacent seat. He was agitated with the dull babysitting assignment, and wanted nothing more than to be done with the task. Other officers on his squad were fulfilling more exciting duties and he wanted to be a part of it, but first he had to deal with the situation at hand. The officer watched as the doctor entered an elevator; he stood and headed toward Genesis' room.

***

"Let's see about the one located in New York," requested Lieutenant Satchel. His reports were almost complete, he'd spent weeks testing subjects from around the country. After today, he was sure he would have enough data to take to Washington, DC.

"Okay, let's get a reading on this one," stated the technician. The monitor displayed a woman located in a hospital setting. They watched the screen. "I'll activate her when she comes into contact with another person."

"God help whomever that may be."

***

Genesis sat on the bed feeling deflated. She stood and gazed out the window, her objective was to find an escape from captivity. The room door opened abruptly; a police officer stood at the threshold. He was frustrated with the delay tactics used by the doctor and felt the job should have been an easy *tag and bag* operation. It was now a long and drawn out episode.

"Miss Rodriguez, I'm with the New York City Police Department. I am here to read your Miranda rights. You are being placed under arrest for drug possession and unclaimed cash found in your apartment."

"You can't be in here! I am under the care of this hospital." Her voice was loud. She hoped to draw attention from passersby in the corridor.

"That's where you're wrong. I am arresting you and getting you out of here. I'm tired of playing games with this uppity doctor." The officer retrieved handcuffs from his utility belt. "You have the right…" The officer was unprepared for what happened next.

An alarming sensation of heat consumed Genesis' body. A bitter metallic taste lingered on her tongue, her heart rate soared and she closed her eyes. When they opened, she stared in disbelief at an unknown entity. The officer was no longer apparent, a creature with furry skin and strands of hair matted to the body stood before her. The creature held a strange weapon, one that was unfamiliar. The beast swung the menacing object toward her. Genesis reacted by ducking under the projection of the thrusted weapon. With a closed fist, she struck the subject in the solar plexus region. The blow impaired the creature's breathing and sent it clashing against a wall. She grabbed the creature's head and twisted the neck at an unnatural angle. The creature's movement stopped; the swift motion killed him instantly. The creature's body was limp; spittle streamed from the side of its mouth. Without hesitation, Genesis stripped out of her hospital gown and placed on the creature's skin.

***

"I've seen enough! It's almost as if the neuro-agent in the bloodstream has the ability to spike changes in the test subject's strength." Lieutenant Satchel's attention was glued to the monitor.

"You're correct, our studies conclude there are more effects. The full report is inconclusive mainly because data is being received as we continue. As stated, the possibilities are unlimited."

18.

The realization of past events were still vague to Zesty as she drove on a quiet residential block. She noticed the sky displayed a chromatic spectrum of colors. The force of the inflated airbag left her face bloodied and bruised. She exited the vehicle in front of Cheryl's home. Zesty sighed before knocking on the door, a light illuminated in the foyer just as the door curtains briefly parted. The locking mechanism resonated in the quiet setting before the door opened to a sleep-deprived figure wearing a pink terrycloth robe over a night gown. Cheryl's hair was wrapped in a blue silk scarf, her feet were stuffed in a pair of pink rabbit-ear slippers. Seeing her friend's condition awakened her fully.

"W-what happened to you?" Cheryl reached out and gently escorted her friend into the house. "Come in." Cheryl scanned the street in both directions before closing the door. She'd noticed an unfamiliar vehicle parked in front of the house.

Cheryl ushered Zesty into the bathroom. "What happened to you? I leave you for a little while and look at you. Did those hoodlums come back and attack you?" Zesty shook her head as a response. Cheryl applied a cold compress to Zesty's nose to stop the bleeding. "Who's responsible for this?"

Glassy-eyed, Zesty stared at her image in the mirror. Her mind recalled the event with clarity. "It was Stax!"

"Stax?"

"Yeah, he came to the club just as I was leaving." Cheryl listened to her friend without interruption. "I confronted him about the attack. He didn't deny it, but became angry. I entered my vehicle and drove away before anything else could ensue. He followed me. The next thing I realized, he drove his vehicle into me from the rear and pushed me into a ditch. I lost control and wrecked my vehicle. When the opportunity came, I maced him…" Zesty was overwhelmed with emotions.

"What's wrong?" The two gazed into one another's eyes.

"The funny thing is I wasn't upset. I was just going to come here to tell you what happened. I thought about calling the police, but everything changed. A strange feeling overcame me, one I've never experienced. I mean it felt as if a spell engulfed me. I thought I was experiencing a stroke or something. Then a bitter metallic taste filled my mouth. After that everything became a blur. All I can remember was finding Stax on the ground, and I was standing over him. He was dead. My vehicle was disabled so I took his…"

"You mean to tell me you drove his vehicle here?"

"Yeah, what else was I suppose to do? Stay there?" Zesty became irate.

"Okay, don't get upset. We'll figure this thing out together. The first thing we have to do is to get you out of those soiled clothes." Cheryl changed her attire. Fifteen minutes later, they were dressed in dark jeans and sweaters. Cheryl drove the sedan while Zesty sat in the passenger seat giving directions. They were headed to the scene of the incident. Cheryl wanted to be sure Stax was dead before continuing with the next part of the plan. The vehicle stopped behind the wreckage, the skyline was illuminated by scintillating stars in the ethers. Cheryl realized traffic would soon increase with commuters heading to work. Cheryl and Zesty exited the vehicle; both stood over Stax's lifeless body. He was faced up on damp marsh; rigor mortis had set in. Cheryl made a decision.

"Let's get all of your belongings. Hurry!" Zesty complied to the request. Cheryl removed the license plates and any other identification items she could find, having a mechanic for a brother gave her the knowledge. Cheryl reached underneath the vehicle and cut the fuel line. She tossed a match under the car, causing flames to ignite and engulf the body.

After securing the incriminating evidence from Zesty's vehicle, the sedan owned by Stax was driven into Lake Ontario. They watched the vehicle submerge into the mirky water.

19.

The basketball team members ran frantically through back streets. Damian took the lead and headed toward a recreational park. The guys flopped onto a bench breathless; their chests heaved from exhaustion.

"What was that all about?" asked Dexter. Perspiration cascaded from his forehead.

"I don't know. I do know we're in big trouble. We literally murdered those guys," stated Damian.

"I-I don't know what came over me. It was as if I wasn't in control of my actions." Stan studied his trembling hands.

"I experienced a heat flash and the next thing I remember is running." Chuck sat hunched over as he struggled to breathe.

"I remembered tasting something bitter." Damian stood. "I don't know what's going on. One thing is for sure, we are murderers. I think we better put some distance between us and this town."

"Where would we go? I don't know any other place," said Dexter.

"He's right, besides we have no money," stated Stan.

"I don't know about you guys, but I am going home to pack a few things. I'm getting out of here. I don't want to spend the rest of my life in a prison cell," said Damian.

"Me neither."

"Nor am I."

"I really think we should separate," said Rufus.

"No, we're family. We should remain together. If you guys agree we can meet at Wilson High School in one hour," suggested Damian. Everyone separated the park using different exits.

***

Stan, Dexter, Rufus, and Chuck arrived at the rear of Wilson High School. They arrived at different intervals anxiously. Damian being the only absentee caused major concern. The guys became unsettled because the plan was his idea.

"Do you think he got pinched?" asked Dexter. The others gazed at one another dumbfounded.

"What are we gonna do now?" asked Stan.

Chuck displayed nervousness. "I say we give him a few more minutes." He glanced at his wristwatch. "Then we move out."

"We can't stay here, it's too dangerous," stated Rufus.

Everyone's attention was adverted toward the roadside as an unfamiliar vehicle slowly approached. The occupants inside the vehicle were obscured from sight because of dark tint on the windows. The guys watch keenly as they prepared to bolt within a second notice. Police was the first thought that came to their minds. The vehicle came to a full stop; the passenger side window descended. Everyone cautiously gazed into the vehicle. Apprehension was replaced with joy.

"Damian!" exclaimed Dexter. He was ecstatic to see his friend. The rest of the guys rushed toward the vehicle.

"Get in," invited Damian.

The group was on their way toward the interstate. Everyone displayed excitement. Damian smiled as he controlled the vehicle.

"Where did you get this?" asked Stan. He sat next to Damian in the front passenger seat. The luxurious interior felt comfortable to everyone.

"I borrowed it from my stepdad; he's home asleep. I dislike the way he treats me; this is retribution." The explanation produced laughter from the group.

"I can imagine his expression when he awaken," said Dexter.

"Even worst, how about when he finds out you and his wheels are gone." The statement by Stan caused more laughter to ensue.

They traveled on an interstate heading southwest. The closest city was Ohio. The excitement of the reunion wore off as reality set in. The guys were quiet and in deep thought, the only sound was from the engine and the tires moving upon the asphalt. The group were experiencing a common emotion called regret, they were overwhelmed with the fact of an uncertain future. Each person once had high hopes of making it to the pros to play ball. The lingering thoughts of being fugitives became the new reality.

Damian broke the silence. "How much cash do we have collectively?"

The question returned the group from their daydreams. Simultaneously, they checked their pockets for cash.

"I have forty dollars," said Dexter.

I have thirty two dollars," stated Stan.

"I only have twenty five," retorted Chuck.

"Man we need more money."

Rufus interjected, "I have about five hundred dollars." The statement gained everyone's attention. "There's more, but I can only access that amount a day from the automated teller machine."

Damian turned his head from the road to take a quick glance at Rufus. "What are you talking about?"

"I'm talkin' 'bout this..." He produced a bank card.

"Where did you get it?"

"It's my moms. She told me to retrieve fifty dollars before all of this took place. I was suppose to bring it home with me after school."

Stan looked back at Rufus. "Man you can't do that."

"After she hears about what happened on the evening news, it won't matter much. I think she would want me to do whatever to be safe. The only thing I feel bad about is letting her down. I had plans on helping her after getting into the pros." His voice trailed off as disappointment lingered.

"Okay, we'll have to hit the first automatic teller machine we come across. We have to do it fast before the card gets flagged. It's too risky going into a bank, we don't know how much information is out there."

"You're right Damian," agreed Rufus.

***

Toledo was the first big city the group encountered on their journey; they stopped at Evergreen Mall. Damian instructed the others to remain in the vehicle while he and Rufus headed into the mall. The interior was massive, automated teller machines were located on the lower mezzanine. Damian kept watchful eyes on patrons while Rufus' back was turned. Minutes later they returned to the vehicle five hundred dollars richer.

"Well? How did it go?" asked Dexter.

"Everything is good."

Damian started the engine and steered the vehicle onto the roadway. The interior of the vehicle was eerily quiet as each person were trapped in their own thoughts. Damian turned left onto a main street. As the vehicle stopped at an intersection, staccato chirps erupted from behind. The abrupt loud noise changed everyone's perspective. A police cruiser emergency lights were illuminated.

Damn! Damian gazed in the rear view mirror. He sighed quietly as an array of thoughts entered his mind.

"What happened?" questioned Dexter.

"What did you do?" asked Stan.

"I didn't do anything. Everybody just remain cool and let me handle this." Damian tried to sound reassuring. He gazed the police cruiser in his rear view mirror and made sure not to make any sudden movements.

Two police officers exited the cruiser simultaneously. Damian watched as they unfastened the safety latches on their holstered weapons. They approached from the rear on opposite sides of the vehicle. Damian stared straight ahead and mentally processed a contingency plan of escape if the need arose. Aviator sunglasses covered the officer's eyes on the driver side. He motioned for the window to descend. Damian slowly reached for the switch. The windows on both sides of the vehicle descended as outside noise filled the interior.

"Is there a problem officer?" Damian kept his hands on the steering wheel. *Maybe this was a bad idea.*

The officer removed his eyewear and gazed at the driver. "I stopped you because your hazards are flashing. In my training that could mean a sign of distress. Is everything all right?" His partner peered into the interior from the passenger side window at the other occupants.

"Everything is fine officer. I had no idea they were on."

The officer studied the exterior of the vehicle for a moment. "This is a nice vehicle. Is it yours?"

"No officer, it belongs to my stepdad. He let me use it. We're returning from a campus game as victors. We're high school students. We play varsity ball."

"Yeah? Who did you play against?"

"Toledo High School, we beat them by six."

The officer glanced at the license plates. "You're a pretty good ways from home. Do you have a driver license and registration?

"Yes…" Damian reached into the glove compartment for the requested documents. He knew where Kenny kept them. Retrieving the documents, he slowly reached into his own pocket for his driver's license, and handed the paperwork to the officer.

Crackling static from the dispatcher on the officer's two-way radio resonated on the busy street. Passing motorist glanced at the scene, passersby stared with curiosity. Some stopped and gawked at the officers. One man recorded the scene with his cellphone. The officer received the documents. "I'll have to call it in. It should only take a few minutes." The dispatcher's voice exploded over the airwaves. *All units, we have a 1-8-7 in progress. Officers need assistance. Mayfield and Evergreen.* The officer stepped back a few feet from the vehicle as he spoke into the microphone fastened to his uniform. "This is unit 5-1-7 in response to 1-8-7 at Mayfield and Evergreen. ETA seven minutes. Roger out!" *Affirmative Unit 5-1-7* The response from the dispatcher was followed by a high-pitch squelch noise in the background. "That's us Rick," stated the officer to his partner. He returned Damian's documents and raced to catch up to his partner at the cruiser. Tires squealed as the cruiser sped away. Everyone in the sports utility vehicle were relieved.

"I now believe it! There must be a higher power because I was praying something fierce," stated Stan.

"That was a close call. Let's get outta here." Damian steered the vehicle onto the interstate.

20.

Dressed as an officer, Genesis exited the secured wing in the hospital. She was plagued by a mental tug-of-war. Not believing her actions, she fought to remain calm and collected. *There has to be an explanation.* A strange inkling gnawed at her conscious, she sensed an outside stimuli was responsible. *I can't go back to the apartment, it's too dangerous. There are probably police waiting to arrest me for killing one of their own.* She realized the dangers that lurked. *I have to get out of these clothes.* Genesis hesitated to cross a street when she noticed a little boy with a ball embraced in his arm; the mother grasped onto his hand. The scene caused her to reflect on the past. Vivid recollections of the previous day flooded her memory, the hindsight caused her to shutter. Carlos' image lingered. She wanted to stop and cry, but realized it would draw unnecessary attention. Dull pangs unexpectedly enveloped in the core of her abdomen. Genesis realized she hadn't ingested food in quite some time. A diner loomed ahead in the distance, delightful aromas associated with breakfast was prominent. Another dilemma occurred, she had no money. Genesis reached into the jacket pocket and felt an object. She stared at a wallet belonging to the murdered officer. The rationalization of being a killer was profound. *I'm a cop killer.* Inside the billfold was a photograph of two children and a lady. Genesis figured it to be the officer's family. Guilt lingered in her mental. *I've caused them grief, and I don't even know them.* The wallet contained credit cards and cash. Genesis entered the diner and took a seat at the counter. The waitress, a middle-aged woman with brunette hair approached. Her uniform was black with white lace trimming.

"What can I get for you dear?"

Genesis glanced at the menu. "I'll have the breakfast deluxe with tea instead of coffee." The waitress went to fill the order. Genesis studied the exits and the patrons in the diner. The place wasn't busy, only five patrons were sitting at different locations enjoying meals. *Okay, think Gen!* Her mind scanned available options.

"Here you go sweetie." The waitress placed a meal in front of Genesis. "Enjoy." She walked away to attend to another customer.

Genesis devoured her breakfast and finished with a fresh glass of orange juice. The hunger pain subsided. She realized time was of an essence. *A cop killer doesn't have a chance in New York City.* Genesis dabbed her lips with a napkin and stood. She placed money on the table as the waitress approached.

"Gone so soon? You must have a busy day ahead being an officer and all."

"I guess you can say that. The meal was delicious."

"Thank you honey. I don't know if anyone's ever told you. You are too pretty to be a crime fighter. Take my advice honey; life is short. Nothing is going to change this world, or the way people view things. Get yourself a nice guy and settle down. Have a few kids; you'll be better off." The waitress gestured with a knowingly wink.

"Thank you. I'll consider the advice." Genesis headed out of the door and entered a small boutique. Clothed mannequins were erected around the shop displaying the latest fashions. Other clothing hung above and around the store on decorative displays.

"Hello officer, how may I help you?" The proprietor was a middle-aged woman dressed in the latest fashion. She wore an over-abundance of makeup.

"Yes, I'm looking for something in a pants outfit. I have an appointment after work, and I need something for casual moonlighting."

"Let's go to the back and see what we can find."

Twenty minutes later, Genesis exited the shop a with a boutique's signature plastic bag. Her mind contemplated her next move and entered a subway station. The low lighting below ground was perfect cover. She made her way to a restroom and exited wearing the newly purchased outfit. She placed the uniform carried in the plastic bag into a trash receptacle, and boarded a northbound train heading uptown.

***

Dr Baden was perplexed with his findings. The results from the blood test baffled him. What puzzled him most was an uncommon element found in Genesis' bloodstream. Using centrifugal force, he was able to separate the foreign matter from the blood. Dr Baden sent the unfamiliar substance to the toxicology lab on the third floor. It was all he could do at the moment.

The public address system sounded throughout the building. *Dr Baden, room seven thirteen. Stat!* The message was repeated in an urgent manner.

The doctor realized it was Genesis' room. *Now what?* He hurried down the corridor toward the elevator. Dr Baden exited to a corridor filled with police activity. A staff nurse approached and filled him in on the current situation.

"He's on the floor dead and Genesis Rodriguez is missing, she must have gotten pass security dressed in the officer's uniform. There's a manhunt out for her arrest. God help her."

"Thank you nurse." Dr Baden continued toward the room, but was intercepted by a large man of African-American descent. The man was neatly groomed and wore a dark-blue two-piece suit, gray shirt with no tie. He retrieved his identification.

"My name is Detective Walters. I'm from the 77th Precinct, Homicide Division." He retrieved a notepad from his pocket and fumbled through a few pages. "You are Dr Baden I presume? I understand Genesis Rodriguez was under your care."

"Yes, Miss Rodriguez is my patient."

"Yes, I've heard." The statement was delivered sarcastically. "I also heard she was under your care and you intervened; preventing the slain officer from doing his duty. Why is that?" He studied Dr Baden's reactions.

Dr Baden understood the implication, he remained calm and professional. "First of all, the patient was under heavy duress. She is suffering from psychosis, an emotional disorder. She saved the life of a child. Afterward, she witnessed her boyfriend being ran over by a high speed vehicle."

"She killed one of my officers. I hardly feel sympathetic toward her at the moment doctor. Do you have a registration on her?"

"Yes, my nurse will help you with that. Is there anything else I can help you with detective?"

The detective shook his head. "No, that will be all for now. If there's anything else, we'll be in touch."

21.

Dr Baden entered his office and sat behind the desk feeling emotionally consumed. He replayed his encounter with Genesis and didn't detect any irregularities in her demeanor that would have triggered her to commit murder. *No, there has to be something I'm overlooking.* A set of metal balls were displayed atop his desktop. The lustrous smooth steel balls aided him when in deep contemplation. He twirled the balls in his hand; the symmetric design and vibrational friction stimulated his hand and mind. Dr Baden gazed out the window; his mind engaged in other thoughts. *What am I not noticing?* Although he didn't actually know Genesis personally, he did know murder didn't fit into the scheme of things. *What pushed her?* An idea formulated; he stood and rushed out the door.

The toxicology laboratory was a mid-level operation with seven technicians assigned to the department. The area was equipped with the latest test machines on the market. A technician peered into the lenses of a microscope, his hair and facial features were obscured with protective gear to maintain a sterile environment. Separated by a partition, Dr Baden tapped on the glass. His need for attention was immediately recognized by the technician with a nod. Shortly after, the two were in a staff lounge area conversing over coffee. A delightful aroma of fresh food waft through the air.

"I see why you were perplexed with the finding. My discovery also had me bewildered. You said this substance was extracted from your patient's bloodstream?" asked Paul Townsend. Paul was a resident technician. He was mild mannered with distinct features such as, black hair, hazel eyes, and dimples that formed on his cheeks when he smiled.

"Yes, please don't leave me in suspense."

"Forgive me." He gestured with his hand. "This substance doesn't exist, at least not yet."

"I don't understand." Dr Baden sipped hot beverage.

"Neither do I. After cross references were done, three isolated compounds that should never meet were discovered. All I can tell you is further investigations came back void of information because it is said to be highly classified. I don't have the government clearance to investigate any further. Truthfully, it seems clandestine. I don't think I want to know what's going on." He sipped his coffee. "There's one other thing I was able to distinguish. There's an ink residue with particles of thandiasine, a highly restricted nerve agent."

"Thank you Paul. I appreciate your service."

***

Tattoo

Lieutenant Satchel gazed at the green dots on the screen, the location zeroed in on Arizona. A technician approached.

"Lieutenant Satchel there's a telephone call for you. It's from Washington DC."

Lieutenant Satchel stood from behind the console and followed the technician to a secure telephone and picked up the receiver. "Hello? This is Lieutenant Satchel." The lieutenant listened attentively without interruptions. He was being notified about an inquiry into a highly classified substance; a compound strictly accessed by the United States government. It was explained to the lieutenant the compound was linked to the i-Ink Project. "Yes sir, I will handle the situation." The line was disconnected, he replaced the receiver on the cradle. A thought occurred; he picked up the receiver and dialed.

***

Paul Townsend returned to his office after speaking with Dr Baden. He noticed his desktop was piled high with documents and toxicology reports. Paul rubbed the tiredness from his eyes. A knock came to the door. "You may enter."

A middle-aged man wearing a janitor uniform entered pushing a trash cart. "Just taking out the trash don't let me disturb you."

Paul studied the janitor and noticed he wasn't the regular. "Where's Ralph? He usually works this floor."

"I'm not sure. All I know is they assigned me to this area temporarily." The janitor began emptying small trash cans into his cart.

Paul reached under his desk where he kept a trash can. It was filled with shredded paper. "I have one right here."

The janitor approached Paul from behind. A ring was worn on the janitor's index finger. He twisted the ring one hundred eighty degrees where a poisonous micro-spike protruded from the ring. The janitor approached Paul from the rear and slapped him on the back of the neck. Paul Townsend's body went limp immediately and slumped over the desk. The janitor returned the ring back to its former position and calmly guided his trash cart out of the office. The ring contained an undetectable syringe filled with a mixture of compounds. Carbon, nitrogen, and potassium was amongst them. The chemical in the commercial industries was called cyanide. The dose travelled in the bloodstream undetected. The obscurity was great because it was camouflaged by natural element in the body. On the surface it appeared the victim died of a massive heart attack.

22.

Cheryl and Zesty concocted a story that would sound believable before entering a police station located in the downtown section of Detroit. The precinct was active with staff escorting defendants to different locations. Cheryl made an inquiry to a desk officer who eyed the ladies delightfully.

"Excuse me, we would like to report a stolen vehicle."

The officer pointed toward the right. "You see those doors? You go through them and up one flight. On your left is where you want to be."

Cheryl and Zesty headed toward the instructed destination; the noise level subsided. A corridor came into view with a stained glass door etched with letters spelling Grand Theft Auto Division. The ladies entered into an active scene. Rows of desks were manned by personnel working on cases. No one took notice as they entered. The first desk was manned by a young man concentrating on a document.

Cheryl found him to be cute. "Uhmm…" She feigned as if clearing her throat, an act to gain his attention.

He looked up from his paperwork. "I'm sorry, what can I do for you?"

Cheryl noticed a name plate on his desk. "We would like to report a stolen vehicle."

"Please have a seat. I'll need to ask you a few questions and issue you a copy of a report to provide to your insurance provider." Cheryl and Zesty sat on wooden chairs adjacent to the desk. "What type of vehicle are we talking about?" Officer Steven Richardson recorded the information onto his database. Twenty minutes later, Cheryl and Zesty exited the police station. Zesty, who was once subdued by the ordeal, returned to her natural spirited self. They sat at a luncheon counter enjoying hot pastrami sandwiches made on pumpernickel rye bread. Provolone cheese topped the delightful meal along with two large glasses of orange juice.

"I want to thank you again for saving my ass Cheryl. I know it's been a regular event concerning me."

Cheryl washed down a mouthful of food before replying. "You don't have to say that to me."

"I still can't place my finger on what caused this to happen. You know I'm not a violent person."

"Remember, fear and adrenaline is a powerful natural mixture. Don't be so hard on yourself. Even you said he tried to hurt you. Running you off of the road the way he did could have killed you. From the look of the wreckage, I'd say you're lucky to be alive.

"Okay, what's next?"

"Call the insurance agency and wait for your big fat check in the mail. Get yourself a new vehicle because if you think I'm chauffeuring you all over town you've got another thing coming." Cheryl couldn't sustain a serious demeanor and burst with laughter.

Zesty also laughed heartily. "That sounds like a plan."

23.

Kenny Washington headed toward the front door to pick up the morning newspaper from the porch, he read the headline caption. *The president puts his foot in his mouth again.* Suddenly, a sensation of nausea was pitted in his core. His heart struggled to pump blood throughout his system. The newspaper dropped from his grasp as perspiration seeped from his pores. "Oh hell no!" Kenny didn't want to believe what he witnessed. His vehicle was no longer in sight; the parking spot was vacant. He entered the house and hurried toward the bedroom, he moved cautiously not wanting to awaken Clair. *Maybe I left the keys in the ignition.* He glanced at the night stand, the place where his keys were kept. The item was missing. He noticed his wallet was in place. *What the hell is going on?* Anxiety overcame his emotions. "Damn!" The outburst awakened Clair.

"W-what is it? What are you doing?" Clair's voice was groggy. She yawned and sat up in bed.

"Nothing honey, I'm sorry to have awakened you. Please, go back to sleep." Kenny headed into the living room and picked up the telephone receiver. A thought arose. He returned the receiver onto the cradle and headed toward Damian's bedroom.

The door hinges squeaked as he eased open the bedroom door. Light from the hall flooded the darkened room creating a shadowy figure of himself against the wall. Kenny focused his attention toward the bed. *What the hell is going on?* Damian's bed was unoccupied. The sight angered Kenny. "That rotten little bastard!" He rushed from the bedroom, picked up the wall-mounted telephone, and placed a call to the police. The dispatcher's questions agitated him, his voice rose in tone. "Yes, I'm sure it's stolen."

Clair entered into the living room wearing a terrycloth robe, her hair was covered with a black satin scarf. The excitement of the telephone conversation fully awakened her. "What's going on?"

Kenny Washington nodded in acknowledgement and pointed to the receiver as he communicated with the dispatcher. When the call was concluded, he replaced the receiver on the cradle and gave attention to Clair. "The truck had been stolen."

"What?"

"Damian isn't in his room. His bed looks as if it hasn't been slept on all night."

"Oh my God!" Her hand went to her mouth as if to stifle a sound. Clair rushed toward Damian's room with Kenny in tow. "Where do you think he is?" Apprehension overwhelmed her.

"I don't know. The keys to the vehicle are missing from the night stand."

"Maybe the truck isn't stolen. Why didn't you wait before calling it in?" She gazed into his eyes.

"I wasn't sure."

"Maybe he's out with a girlfriend trying to impress or something. He's only a teenager. I bet you've done stupid things also when you were a teen."

Kenny hated the fact she always tried to protect Damian. "It's still wrong."

"I agree, but with the police out searching for the vehicle he could be arrested or even killed. His chances of getting a good education will be finished. Please, call them back and tell them the truck has been returned."

"No, I will not!" exclaimed Kenny. He was obviously angered. Clair rushed from the room feeling distraught. Tears flow down her cheeks.

A knock was at the door. Kenny opened the door to see two police officers standing on the porch.

"Thank you for coming, please come in."

They sat in the kitchen making out an incident report. Kenny intentionally obscured the fact about Damian being absent. After the report was completed, the officers exited with promise of looking into the matter. One officer turned toward Kenny. "In the past, most vehicles were stripped beyond recognition."

Kenny Washington entered the bedroom to find Clair dressing in a hurried manner. She was obviously upset. "Don't tell me you're angry."

She stopped in mid motion and stared directly into his eyes. "Are you kidding? Not once did you mention Damian being missing. Don't you care?"

"You said so yourself reporting it would make things worse. Especially, if he's caught inside the vehicle."

"I see it didn't stop you from making the report."

"Clair you're always trying to protect that boy whether he's right or wrong."

"Exactly what a mother is suppose to do." Her words were defiant.

"Do you have any idea of the ramifications of not reporting the theft? Then to find out it wasn't him and the real thieves trashed the vehicle. My insurance wouldn't be worth squat."

Clair placed on her jacket. "While you worry about your precious machine, I'm going out to look for my son." Without another word, Clair headed out of the door. Kenny fumed with anger.

24.

Damian drove Kenny's sports utility vehicle most of the day and partially into the evening. Stan relieved him periodically. The only discontinuances in the journey were for fuel, restroom breaks, and the stretching of the limbs. Hours into the trip, the group drove through Pennsylvania. They continued toward New York State. A town called Newburgh is where they stopped for fuel. The guys exited the vehicle in effort to stretched their limbs. Damian was at the pump refueling the vehicle when Stan approached.

"Man you look exhausted! You need to get some rest. In fact, we all could use a shower and a change of clothing."

"I feel you," retorted Damian. "I take that back, I smell you." Laughter ensued.

The journey continued on the main street. The group stopped at a motel. Damian exited alone and entered the main lobby to purchased a room. The guys entered through the rear exit, it was a way to save money instead of purchasing multiple rooms. Everyone showered and changed clothes. Dexter went to the nearest restaurant to order take-out food.

"The little cash we have won't last much longer, we have to come up with a plan," stated Stan to the group.

"This room is rented for eight hours, I suggest we get some rest. Then we can figure out our next move," replied Damian. Everyone was in agreement.

***

Two local guys watched an unfamiliar vehicle enter the parking lot of a motel. They observed the situation from afar, watching a group exit and head inside the building. Similar events led the observers to believe the group were from out of town. It was a known fact people arrived to take over the drug business in the area. The last group was chased out of town with guns blazing.

"You see that man?" questioned an observer. He wore designer eyewear and a knock-off baseball cap.

"Yeah, the plates are from Detroit. Maybe they're new players on the block trying to make a name for themselves. You remember what happened to the last crew who came 'round here."

"Look at those wheels. We can get a pretty penny for that vehicle. After we get the cash, we can go and tell the others about the newcomers on the block. Com' on," said his partner.

Dressed in black jeans and black hooded sweatshirts, the observers gained access into the sports utility vehicle. Within seconds, they eased out of the parking lot without being noticed.

***

Clair probed in the streets for Damian, and visited all the houses of his friends. The search revealed his teammates were also missing. Parents of the teammates were equally worried and collectively decided to go to the authorities.

Kenny paced in the living room trying to figure out what Damian's intentions were. His anger subsided as time passed, and an idea formulated. Kenny picked up the telephone dialed.

"Mobilnet? I would like to report my vehicle missing. I need to have tracking initiated to locate its whereabouts. I also wish to have the engine shut off electronically if it's in motion." Kenny began answering a barrage of questions about the vehicle identification numbers. He was placed on hold while the Mobilnet operator searched the databanks for information. She returned shortly afterward.

"Sir your vehicle has been located in New York State."

"New York State?"

"Yes, it is in motion. Would you like the engine terminated and the authorities notified?"

"Yes, I would like the authorities notified before the engine is terminated. I want the culprits arrested."

"As you wish Mr Washington. You will be notified when the task is completed." The line was disconnected.

Tattoo

Kenny stared at the receiver as if it were a foreign object, his mind contemplated what was happening. A smile ensued. *I got you now Damian. I'll show you not to take my property without permission.* Another thought occurred. *Maybe now your mother will see how much of a brat you really are.*

After making formal missing persons reports, all five parents exited the police station worried out of their minds. Clair decided to head home, hoping Damian would be there.

***

The stolen sports utility vehicle headed down Main Street. "Man we're gonna get paid for this ride. Check the glove compartment," stated the guy with the baseball cap. He was the obvious leader.

"There's a few…" Loud chirps from a police cruiser pierce through the night. Red and blue lights danced atop. The occupants of the stolen vehicle were startled.

"What did you do?"

The driver looked at his partner nervously. "I didn't do nuthin'."

"Why did you stop?"

"I didn't, the damn thing just shut off!"

Two police officers approached the sports utility vehicle with their weapons drawn. The aftermath resulted with the arrest of the two perpetrators for possession of stolen property. They were escorted to the rear compartment of a cruiser. A tow truck appeared on the scene to impound the stolen vehicle.

***

Clair entered the quiet house to find Kenny sitting in the living room staring into oblivion. The sound returned him from his reverie. He stood and faced Clair. "Did you discover anything?"

Clair gestured with a shrug. "No, I was hoping to find him here. I filled out a missing person report. The parents of the other teammates were also worried because their kids are missing also. Did he call?"

"No." Kenny approached Clair and embraced her. "I'm sorry about earlier."

"So am I."

"I called the Mobilnet company to get a tracking on the whereabouts of the vehicle. They spotted the vehicle in New York State."

"New York?"

"I had the same reaction. Yes, they will electronically shut down the engine with police assistance. I'm sorry, I had to."

The telephone rang before Clair could respond. Kenny was the closest to the receiver. He quickly answered before the first ring expired.

"Hello? Yes this is Mr Washington…" Kenny listened to the report. "Okay, thank you." The line was disconnected.

"Well? What is it?" Clair was obviously anxious.

"They stopped the vehicle at a location in Newburgh, New York. Two people in custody."

"Oh my God!" Clair became frantic. Mixed emotions permeated her being. She truly hoped it wasn't her son held captive in a foreign state. She began missing Damian even more, she wanted him home at any cost. "Okay, let's go to New York."

"First, I have to call the New York State authorities to make sure it's Damian." He picked up the receiver and dialed. "Yes sir, I'll be there soon to pick up the vehicle. Thank you." Kenny replaced the receiver and faced Clair. "They have the vehicle. It wasn't Damian nor any of his friends apprehended. They said the guys in custody are local thugs."

Thank goodness. Clair felt relieved.

25.

A public address system summoned Dr Baden to the third floor. *Now what?* A nurse intercepted his path in efforts to gain his signature on a patient profile document as he headed toward the elevator bank. Dr Baden exited the car onto a busy floor. *What's going on today?* The presence of police officers sparked his curiosity. Dr Baden spotted Detective Walters as he approached the chaotic scene. Dr Baden noticed the detective's suit, it was similar to the one he wore earlier, differing with a grey shirt. His hands were covered with latex gloves.

"Dr Baden."

"Detective Walters."

"It looks as if there's a pattern being set here in your hospital." The detective studied the doctor's reaction.

"I don't understand." Dr Baden glance around the corridor.

"What's going on here?"

"Another murder. This time a technician named Paul Townsend."

"Paul?"

"Yes, he was found dead at his desk. The obvious reason is a heart attack. We'll have to perform an autopsy to determine what is the real culprit."

"I don't understand, I just visited with him a couple of hours prior. He seemed fine."

"We know, the corridor camera picked you up entering his office. You could also be seen exiting alone. We noticed a janitor entering and leaving. We are following up on that as we speak."

Dr Baden posture stiffened. "What are you insinuating?"

"Facts, just facts." Detective Walters placed his hand up as a defensive gesture. "Can you tell me what the two of you talked about?"

"We discussed the test results of a patient. Can I go inside?"

Detective Walters shook his head. "I'm sorry, but that's not possible at the moment. The area is officially a crime scene."

"If that is all, I would like to be excused. I think I'm going to be sick."

"You go on ahead. I'll be in touch." He watched the doctor head down the corridor. *Something is not computing here.*

Dr Baden felt a strange inkling of foul play after receiving the news. He didn't believe in coincidences. *Something is going on and I'm going to find out what it is.* He headed toward the toxicology laboratory.

Inside, he found the sample of the mysterious strain Paul Townsend last worked on. Removing the sample, he headed out of the laboratory.

Dr Baden drove toward an industrial zone and stopped in front of a windowless brick building. The location was a private laboratory the hospital contracted out work to help with backlogged orders. The doctor entered the building and was greeted by familiar faces and a warm reception. He conversed with a laboratory technician named Abu Necthar. The technician, a dark complexion, middle eastern man with puffy eyelids.

"Abu, I need a favor. Can you analyze this specimen and identify the source of the elements?" Dr Baden handed Abu the test tube.

Abu smiled and stared at the specimen. "What is this? A test? Give it to me and come back in an hour."

***

Genesis realized going to the apartment was a bad idea. She entered the university campus through the north-east corridor, and headed toward a bank of lockers. Retrieving a backpack from a locker, she moved through the streets covertly hoping not to be recognized. Aware of the authorities, she exited a local department store armed with a backpack and shopping bags. Genesis hailed a taxicab and was driven to a motel. Inside a second floor room, she closed the drapes and removed the purchased items. Genesis placed the objects methodically upon the bed before entering the bathroom. After cutting and dying her hair, she exited the bathroom and dressed into the new clothing. The garment was a size too small, but perfect for its intended effect. Genesis studied her appearance in the mirror and smiled at the results. Her image resembled that of a male. *This is probably how a butch must feel.* Her feminine clothing was exchanged for a pair of low-cut sneakers, denim jeans, and a dark hooded sweatshirt. A sport cap covered her head. The contours of her body was obscured, giving her the masculine appearance she sought. Genesis traveled to a seedy part of town where she was raised. Cars were parked on both sides of the one-way street. Aggressive barking noise resounded in the distance. Genesis spotted a guy sitting on a brownstone stoop.

"Chuck, I need to holla' at you for a moment."

The guy stared at the stranger using his name, he didn't recognize the person. "I don't know you. How's it you know my name? You police or sumthin'?"

"It's me Genesis!"

Bewildered, he inspected her eyes. Chuck was a firm believer there was no deception in the eyes. "Genesis? Is that really you?"

She smiled. "Yeah, it's me."

"What's up? The last thing I remember you were going to school. You mean to tell me they turned you out that quick? Hell no! You are too beautiful for that crap."

Genesis smiled. "Thank you, it's not what it may seem. I'm in big trouble and I need help."

"What's up?" Chuck was now intrigued. The two were raised in the same area and were close friends.

"I need identification papers to get outta here."

Chuck glanced up and down the block to make sure they weren't being observed. "Com' with me."

They sat in a basement of a two-family house. Genesis gave him an unabridged version of the situation. Chuck was happy to help. He despised authorities mainly because of his many run-ins with the law. Chuck felt he never received a fair deal.

"Okay, take off your hat and stand over there." He pointed to a spot on the floor marked with white chalk. A camera on a tripod was stationed in front. Electronic gadgets were atop a kitchen table. The equipment seemed out of place in the dilapidated building. They waited for the development of the document by way of a special software.

Chuck handed Genesis a replica of an official document. It was a photographed driver's license of her as a male. The name on the document was Dave Mendez.

Genesis was truly impressed and thankful. "Thank you Chuck. I owe you." She reached over and planted a kiss on his cheek.

Chuck backed away playfully. "Hey watch it! I don't want anyone to get the wrong idea. You know what I mean?" He relaxed his wrist as a gesture. "I don't want people to think I'm kissing a guy. If you ever change back, I would be more than happy to oblige."

Genesis laughed. "There's one other thing, I need a burner phone."

Chuck reached into his pocket and handed her an untraceable cellphone. "Use it, then throw it away."

26.

Cheryl drove onto the street where Zesty lived. Zesty's heart felt as if it was going to explode as they neared the house. The sight of police activity alarmed her. Cheryl tried earnestly to hold it together.

"Just stay calm."

They headed toward the house when a uniformed officer approached. "Which one of you is Mrs Crawford?"

"That's me," responded Zesty.

"We have news about your vehicle. It has been located on Interstate 80. We need for you to come down to the station to identify the vehicle."

Zesty looked to Cheryl for guidance. Cheryl nodded and adverted her attention to the officer. "We'll drive ourselves.

The officer shrugged his shoulders apathetically. "Suit yourself." He was indifferent about the situation, his function was to deliver the message.

The precinct was noisy and busy with activity. Defendants were being brought into the station and led to holding areas in chains. Officers were systematically processing defendants one at a time.

Zesty and Cheryl headed toward a desk sergeant. The sergeant called for Officer Steven Richardson.

"Mrs Crawford, I am glad to inform you that your vehicle was recovered. Would you ladies mind coming with me?" He led them to a sub-basement lined with vehicles of every description. Painted yellow lines separated the cars by model. They were led toward the rear where Zesty's vehicle came into view. The vehicle was smashed and burned, the sight of it caused anxiety for Zesty. Cheryl squeezed her arm firmly for support. Zesty's mind vividly recalled the incident, the entire sequences of the events were displayed mentally. Cheryl witnessed a faraway gaze in Zesty's eyes, and nudged her to disconnect from her daydream.

"I'm alright," whispered Zesty.

"Is this your vehicle?" asked Officer Richardson.

"Yes, no. I think so. It's totally damaged and burned beyond recognition. There's no license plate. It's hard to tell."

"We used the information you provided and matched the engine's serial numbers to your registration. You'll have to get the insurance company involved. I'm going to need for you to sign some forms back at the office." Zesty and Cheryl followed.

After the signing, a knock came to the office door. A man dressed in casual attire entered the room. A silver badge hung loosely around his neck.

"Steve, are you finished with Mrs Crawford?"

"As a matter of fact we're all done here."

The officer introduced himself to the ladies as Detective Donald Byrd. He focused his attention toward Zesty. "Mrs Crawford, I need for you to come with me."

"W-what for?" Nervousness enveloped her response.

"I'm with the Homicide Division. The remains of a human being was found at the scene. At the moment we're not able to positively identify the victim, we think foul play is involved. We found two different footprint patterns along with additional tire tracks near the scene. We're speculating murder was committed with the use of your vehicle. We need a statement as to your whereabouts prior to acknowledging your vehicle was stolen."

"I was exiting from my place of employment."

"Is there anyone that can collaborate your story?"

"I can vouch for her," stated Cheryl. "I work with her and I was there."

"Please follow me."

After the inquisition, Zesty and Cheryl were released. Not wanting to be alone, Zesty decided to spend time at Cheryl's apartment. She felt the pangs of guilt for getting her best friend involved in the matter. *What have I gotten us into?*

27

UNITED STATES DEPARTMENT OF DEFENSE CONFERENCE ROOM: A WASHINGTON, DISTRICT OF COLUMBIA

Lieutenant Satchel and four highly decorated government officials sat in a huge conference room. Electronic blinds covered the windows, powerful halogen lights illuminated the enclosure. Placemats, stainless-steel pitchers, and fine crystal glasses were atop a mahogany table. Executives representing the armed forces were present. Each person adorned a uniform that represented a particular branch of service; folders were placed in front of each member. Lieutenant Satchel sat at the head of the table, it was his presentation under review. He displayed data footage from the test subjects in the field.

"Gentlemen, please open your folders. As you can see, extensive research went into this highly classified project. With the tests concluded, we have a ninety-eight percent success rate. That gentlemen is a remarkable achievement. Although the project is clandestine in nature, some of the test subjects have become headline news." The lieutenant hesitated as he noticed the group eyed one another with deep concern. "Not to worry. As you are aware, the movie theater incident where a person fired an automatic weapon on a crowd of moviegoers was documented as a mass shooting. There was another incident where a guy was arrested for eating the face of a person. That was considered a cannibalistic cult encounter. There were a few others, but rest assure none of the infractions can be traced to us."

"Okay," stated the executive officer. His branch of service was the Marines. "Are you confident the program will work in the field?" His name plate read General Carlson. The general was in his mid fifties with splotches of salt and pepper hair.

"I don't see why not. The American people are no different in biological terms. If it works here, I don't see why it would fail to work on our counterparts."

"I say we give it a test run on true subjects," stated the executive officer for the Army. His name plate read General Major Weatherby. He wore a distinguished handlebar mustache, not many officers in the department were allowed to wear facial hair. General Major Weatherby's long term enlistment in the armed service was highly regarded amongst all the branches. The group agreed.

"Then it's all settled."

Lieutenant Satchel's cellphone vibrated as he exited the conference room. He answered the call. "Yes?" He listened attentively without interruption. "I'll take care of it."

***

Dr Baden returned to the laboratory to get the results on the blood samples. Abu Necthar smiled at the sight of the doctor, it thrilled him to showcase his abilities.

"Dr Baden, I'm glad you're here. I have some interesting information for you. Please have a seat. I had to double check it before I was convinced of what I was witnessing." Dr Baden sat while Abu Necthar retrieved some documents from his desk drawer. He sat across from Dr Baden. "I must say this specimen doesn't exist in America. You see this?" He handed the doctor a document. "This substance is called thandiasine. It's a highly restricted nerve agent."

Dr Baden studied the documents Abu explained. A touch of deja' vu entered his mental perception as he heard similar words from his friend Paul Townsend who was now dead. "So how could it wind up in a patient?"

"That I can't answer. I'm as intrigued as you. There's more, I took the liberty to further investigate." He looked around to make sure he wasn't overheard. "My major studies in college included computer science and programming. I took the liberty to find a source. There seems to be only one place on earth to find the base material to make thandiasine. It's a plant that only grows in the Andes mountain of Peru. Records show the only supplier in the entire world has shipped two thousand kilos of the material to the United States." He held up his hand to stop Dr Baden from further questions. "Wait! There's more. Upon further investigation, the shipment was ordered by the defense department and sent to a private laboratory in Great Falls, Montana. What puzzled me is the laboratory is an industrial ink factory."

"Ink?"

"I stumbled upon a government program called i-Ink. It was classified top secret and I was immediately shut out."

"You've done great! Thank you." Dr Baden stood to leave. "Oh yeah, please be careful." He reflected back to Paul Townsend.

Dr Baden tried to make sense of the situation as he drove his vehicle. *i-Ink? I have to find out what this is all about, and how is Genesis Rodriguez involved.*

***

Genesis rode in a taxicab and retrieved the cellphone given to her by Chuck. *I have to find Dr Baden, maybe he knows why I acted irrational.* Genesis felt good about confiding in the doctor because he displayed genuine concern. She recognized his interference earlier to keep the authorities at bay. Genesis dialed a series of numbers and disguised her voice as she connected with the hospital. She impersonated being an executive inquiring about Dr Baden and was immediately connected through the hospital switchboard.

"Hello?" Dr Baden answered his telephone using his hands-free device as he drove. He was surprised to hear the familiar voice on the line. "Genesis? Slow down and tell me your location." He gazed out the window to view his own location. "Can you meet me at Metro Tech? I'll be at the Jay Street entrance."

Genesis was delighted to hear his voice. Although he was a stranger, she felt his sincere presence. "Driver can you take me to Metro-Tech downtown?"

***

Abu Necthar received a call from a home security network claiming his alarm was activated and the authorities were notified. Abu Necthar lived minutes from the laboratory, he entered his vehicle and headed home. Preoccupied in thought, Abu didn't realize a sedan stopped adjacent to him as he waited at a red light on a deserted street. Abu gazed straight ahead waiting for the light to change and didn't see the passenger side window of the sedan descend. For a brief moment, a strange inkling nudged Abu. He eyed the vehicle next to him. Flash fire exploded from a handgun. Abu felt a pinch, then calmness and darkness engulfed his being. Abu was slumped over the steering wheel unmoving and breathless. The traffic light changed to green and the dark sedan moved onward down the quiet street.

28.

Clair Washington sat nervously in the living room. The only sound emitted was from a television broadcasting the local news. Her mind wasn't focused on the news, but on a wall mounted telephone. She hoped Damian would call, hearing his voice meant he was alive. Kenny entered the room.

"Aren't you gonna do something?" Her outburst was more than a question, but a burning anger that brewed inward.

"Yes, maybe I can get a lead on him when I'm in New York."

"I think we should get someone other than the authorities involved. Suppose he's being held captive? Waiting for help from the police could probably be time consuming. "If…" Clair was stunned by the images on the television screen. The evening news broadcasted a breaking news story. Images on the screen were sandy with contrast. A video was taken by an amateur using a cellphone. What held her attention was the image on the screen resembled Damian. The newscaster's voice was barely audible. "Kenny, please turn it up! Hurry!"

...earlier today. It is said the group turned vicious on a rival team with deadly violence. It all stemmed from a friendly game of basketball. The altercation took place at a community recreation center. There's no information as to what caused the onslaught. This amateur video is the only footage of the violent melee. The five men can be seen exiting the recreation center and blending in with the frenzied crowd. Police are now investigating the identity of the group. We will keep you-

Clair reached for the remote and turned off the television. She didn't want to hear anymore. "Can you believe this? How can this be happening?" Her legs failed to give support as she stood. Kenny was there to catch her.

"Easy, let me get you to bed." He placed her in his arms. She began to talk incoherently. Kenny placed her in bed. "Things will be all right."

"How can you say that? That was Damian they spoke about on the news. That's probably why your vehicle is gone. Poor boy was so frightened he fled in it." She sighed. "I'm wondering. If it wasn't them in the vehicle, how did it get to New York? Where are they now?" Clair sobbed from sadness.

Kenny exited the room and returned with a concoction of tea and brandy. "Drink this, it'll help you to unwind." He watched as Clair sipped the warm beverage. Moments later she became drowsy; the effect of the brandy relax her. Kenny waited until she was asleep before exiting the room.

***

The alarm of a wristwatch jarred Damian awake. Tired and drowsy, he made his way toward the bathroom. Damian stepped over Stan who was sleeping on the floor. The cramped room afforded them no amenities. Damian decided to retrieved a pair of pants from the vehicle. He stepped outside onto the parking lot where the vehicle was parked. Total surprise consumed him. Damian glanced around the parking area as realization set in. The vehicle was missing from the place it was once parked. His first thought was a practical joke was being implemented. That notion soon faded as he stood in the empty parking space where the vehicle was last seen. He rushed back into the motel.

"Guys! Wake up!" The group stirred. The sounds of moans were audible. "Someone stole the truck!"

Stan was first at attention. "What do you mean?"

"Just what I said, it's gone."

The guys became alert and rushed outside. Standing on an empty parking spot, mixed emotions of fear and anger surged.

"What are we gonna do?" asked Dexter. He struck his right fist into his left palm; a sign of frustration.

Damian began to pace, his movement stopped as a notion came to mind. He faced the group. "This is what we're going to do. It's not as bad as it seems. Maybe we've been traveling in that vehicle much too long already. Let's get back into the motel and figure things out. I don't think it's safe for us to be out on the streets."

Inside the cramped quarters of the motel room, the guys sat on the bed and floor. Damian stood in the center of the room.

"The money we have will not last long, I think we should keep

115

heading north. Maybe we can get lost in a massive populated place. A huge place like New York City."

"But how are we gonna get there?" asked Stan.

"None of us know anything about stealing a vehicle," retorted Chuck.

"I got it! We'll take a Greyhound bus into New York. It's not that far away. It'll will give us time to think out our next plan."

"Plan? What plan? Where are we going? Why are we running? I don't even know what made us do what we've done." Rufus was confused and agitated. He trembled uncontrollably as tears flowed down his cheeks. "I miss home…" He became emotionally overwhelmed. Everyone were empathetic; they too felt the same sentiment.

29.

A distinctive aroma of almond roasted coffee waft through the air with a potency that awakened Cheryl, it was her favorite blend. Although sleep deprived, she followed the scent into the kitchen. She gazed sleepy-eyed at the wall clock.

"What are you doing up this early? Do you have any idea as to what time it is?" Cheryl saw two breakfast plates on the table. The plates consisted of fried eggs, bacon, toast, and hash brown potatoes.

Zesty sat at the table staring at her best friend as she entered the room, her face produced a smile. "I was just timing you to see how long would you be able to resist my cooking. Sit down and join me."

Cheryl sat. "Did you get any sleep?"

"Very little, to be honest I'm scared. You heard what that detective said about the crime scene. It's as if he knows something isn't right. The questions he asked made me nervous."

Cheryl took a sip of the hot beverage and placed the cup on the table. "He's just fishing, that's what he's trained to do. Only you can hurt you. Remember, I'm involved now, I know you don't want anything to happen to me. Right?"

Zesty looked away. "I'm sorry Cheryl. Nothing like this has ever happened."

"Let's forget about it and eat."

***

Detective Byrd interrogated one of the suspects about the murder of Stax. The suspect's name was Delory Johnson. The reason the detective chose to question him was because it was rumored the defendant was the leader of an infamous group of thugs. The other person was being interrogated simultaneously by another officer. Delroy's dark complexion glistened with perspiration; his eyes shifted constantly under heavy questioning.

Detective Byrd dropped a folder on the desk, a dramatic thud sound effect gave ambiance to the seriousness of the matter. Delroy fidgeted in his seat. The setting was typical, a chipped wooden table divided them, a fluorescent fixture overhead provided artificial lighting. Gloom and hopelessness permeated the room, along with low temperature to cause discomfort. Detective Byrd opened the folder and leafed through the documents. "Delroy, I'm not going to sit here and bullshit you. I can see from your record you're not new to the system. I'm sure you are aware what another blemish on your record would do. You'll be what is considered a career offender. Do you know what that mean?" Detective Byrd didn't wait for an answer. "I'll tell you, life behind bars."

"I-I don't know what you're talking about. I didn't kill Stax! What would I do that for?"

"I'll tell you this…" The detective hesitated for an effect. "When my men get finished working on your partner, I'll bet he'll change his tune. Be smart and save yourself. Remember, a chain is only as strong as its weakest link." Detective Byrd gave him a sly wink.

"I don't know shit!"

"Suit yourself." Detective Byrd gathered the document from the table, stood, and headed out of the room without another word.

Delroy's mind contemplated what his partner was going to say under pressure. He knew from other's experiences how the last man standing took all of the pressure. "Okay!" Detective Byrd released the door knob, turned to face Delroy, and smiled inwardly at his effective tactic. "Stax paid us to rob his girl."

"His girl? Who's his girl? Does she have a name?"

"A dancer that goes by the name Zesty."

Detective Byrd was startled hearing the name. *Things are beginning to make sense.* He continued listening to Delroy's story. *When these guys start talking it's as if you have to put duct tape on their mouths to shut 'em up.*

30.

Misty rain descended covering the streets with a slick sheen. Smoke mixed with ash polluted the air with a rancid stale odor in an industrial area. Spectrum Laboratory is the place where Detective Walters was summoned. The killing of a laboratory technician on a residential street led the detective to the specific locale. It was the technician's place of employment. The detective's initial thought was road rage. Since no witnesses came forward, he suggested it to be a professional hit. The conclusion became prominent because no evidence was left at the scene. Detective Walters questioned co-workers; no one was aware of any threat to Abu Necthar. The staff couldn't imagine anything harmful happening to Abu. The impression the detective received during his investigation was the technician was well liked. Detective Walters discovered that Abu lived a few blocks from the laboratory.

"Could it have been a drug-related incident?" Detective Walters referred to a co-worker named Sandy Miller, the newest edition to the staffing at the laboratory. She graduated from a technical university and was employed by Spectrum Laboratory. Detective Walters noticed her auburn hair naturally matched her eyebrows. She reminded him of a spokeswoman for a fast-food commercial. The detective tried not to stare at her pierced tongue pin.

"No sir, definitely not. Abu wasn't the type. Besides, there's no drugs in this facility. It's not that kind of laboratory. We deal with chemical compound identification. Things such as identifying compounds in blood samples."

"Are there any records that may show the jobs Abu was working on before his untimely death?"

"I'll check." Sandy walked toward Abu's work area with Detective Walters in tow. She opened a logbook. "It says here that Dr Baden came in earlier."

"Dr Baden? Why would Dr Baden come here?"

Sandy saw the surprise expression. "Dr Baden is here quite often. When the hospital is overbooked with orders, they sometimes contract us to handle the overflow."

"I understand. Can you tell me what he was working on?"

She continued reading from the logbook. "It shows test results from a nameless patient." She looked upon the cluttered desk. "He was thinking about something called thandiasine. There's a slash with the word i-Ink. I have no idea what it means."

Detective Walters jotted the information onto a notepad. "Thank you Mrs Miller. You've been a big help."

"I hope you catch the culprits."

***

Metro Tech is an innovative addition to a troubled economy, adding hundreds of jobs to the downtown area. Ground level shops were filled with patrons, the lunch time crowd was already in full swing. Dr Baden sat on a decorative metal bench feigning interest in a newspaper article held close to his face; his eyes searched for Genesis.

Exiting a taxicab, Genesis spotted Dr Baden immediately. Her heart rate soared with hope as she eagerly hurried toward him. The energy she displayed resembled that of a child after seeing a familiar face. Dr Baden stood as she approached and was met with an unexpected embrace.

"Did you find anything useful?"

"Yes and no." He skeptically glanced at a crowd of people. "Com' on, we can't stay here." Dr Baden led Genesis down steps into a subterranean subway system. The sound of mechanical clatter drowned their voices from being overheard. Dr Baden and Genesis sat in a two-seater section of a railcar, the momentum of the train caused involuntarily movement.

"Why didn't we use your vehicle?" asked Genesis.

"I felt it could easily have been traced through my license plates."

"Okay, what did you find out?" Genesis was obviously anxious.

"Anyone inquiring into the matter ended up dead." Genesis placed both her hands to her mouth as if to stifle a scream. "There's more, I noticed you've recently had artwork performed on your body. Can you tell me the name of the tattoo parlor?"

Genesis stared at him perplexed. "Yes, but what does that have to do with anything? The place is called Urban Ink World. They're a new franchise springing up in every neighborhood."

"Exactly when did you get this artwork?"

Genesis thought about the question for a moment. "It was the day before the accident. Carlos just received his tattoo with me urging him." Her voice crackled from painful recollections, she regained her composure and continued. "I remember being in the hospital with a bitter taste in my mouth, prior to a hot flash consuming me. I blanked out afterward. Please believe me, I've never done anything like this. It's not my doing I tell you."

"My guess is you received a highly restricted nerve agent into your bloodstream by way of the ink." Dr Baden went on to explain his findings.

Genesis listened attentively, she sensed being told a science-fiction story from a novel. The doctor's hypothesis was unbelievable. "If what you say is true, what can I do? You said so yourself the compound is highly restricted. Doesn't that mean the government has something to do with it? How else would the stuff make it into the United States? It wasn't me that killed that officer. I have to find a way to prove my innocence."

"We need access to a computer."

Genesis grasped Dr Baden's hand and led him from the subway to the surface. They headed toward a local college. The corridors were active with movement as they headed toward a computer lab.

"This is where it becomes tricky. I am told the company that processed this stuff is outsourced. I gather it's some kind of governmental intelligence project." Dr Baden pressed keys on the keyboard in rapid succession. It was his attempt to fend off any security measures the program provided. His efforts were immediately challenged by a complex security firewall. He tried again and was met with the same unsuccessful fate. He sighed deeply displaying frustration.

Genesis nudged him. "Allow me to try."

Dr Baden exchanged seats with Genesis, he displayed an unsure gesture by shrugging his shoulders. "Suit yourself, but I must warn you, it's no easy task." Genesis concentrated on the screen. "What's wrong?" asked Dr Baden.

"Nothing, I am gaining a feel for it. They are using a Tri-Phi-Serpent coding."

"A what?" Dr Baden was perplexed at the statement.

Genesis glanced at the doctor for an instant, then adverted her attention to the screen. "Never mind, just watch." Using the keyboard, she began entering a series of codes she herself designed. Her speed on the keyboard was more rapid; the screen displayed security pop-ups. No sooner as they appeared, she dismissed the threat. Genesis continued hammering at the security firewall system by adding another equation for the computer to decipher. The computer counteracted with its own measures to secure its data from unregistered intruders. Genesis relentlessly continued pressing keys to override the system. She fired cyber missiles at the security firewall in succession; the projectiles were virtual equations. Dr Baden became alarmed as he watched her gaze at the monitor in deep concentration.

Genesis was mentally inside the computer challenging its logic. Minutes later the program gave in, the security system succumbed to the gauntlet of virtual firepower. The monitor displayed the Spectrum Laboratory interface programming. "Voila!"

"I'm definitely impressed, where did you learn that?"

Genesis' smile exposed pearly white teeth. "In school. Actually, I learned more about hacking from the local neighborhood kids. The only difference in school, you receive technical terminology to what the kids take for granted." They exchanged seats.

Dr Baden processed the information he obtained from Paul Townsend and Abu Necthar. The information led to the Department of Defense. He tried to access the program, and was met with more security interference. Dr Baden gazed at Genesis, his expression resembled that of a sad puppy. "Do you mind?"

Genesis chuckled. "Move over, I get the feeling we're playing musical chairs without the music." After the seat exchange, she added her expertise to the program. She gained access and scooted over to allow Dr Baden control of the program. "There's a three minute time window before it closes. I'm sorry, it's the best that I can do. We're up against the government."

Dr Baden read technical data from the screen. Genesis was lost as to the meaning of the language, compounds, and chemical elements. It was never a strong point in her learning ability. She watched as the doctor read and retained the information to memory. A notion struck as the computer screen went blank. He stood abruptly.

"What's wrong?" Genesis became startled.

"Let's get out of here." He grasped her arm and hurriedly escorted her out of the building. His mind was in overdrive; every unfamiliar face was now a potential threat. The information he received had national security ramifications. Dr Baden felt their lives were in eminent danger. As they exited the campus lobby, they saw men in dark suits hurrying in their directions. Communication earpieces protruding from their ears. The men rushed toward the direction from whence Genesis and the doctor left. Dr Baden flagged a taxicab. The driver of the livery service was a Middle Eastern man with brownish skin. Dr Baden studied his license photograph. "Take us to the Long Island Railroad Station."

"Yes sir."

31.

PORT OF AUTHORITY/BUS TERMINAL
NEW YORK CITY

The group exited the terminal onto a busy city setting with a spectacular view. Passersby moved about displaying no recognition to them. Damian gazed at the abundance of thriving businesses along the streets. Large screens atop massive structures caught their attention.

"I see why they call it the Big Apple," stated Dexter. He was totally in awe.

"Yeah, this is nice," said Stan.

Damian spotted a structure resembling a local precinct in the center of the square. Horseback mounted police were in view. "We have to keep moving. Let's blend in with the crowd and get away from here."

They moved toward a subway station, the sound of trains moving along metal rails crescendoed as they neared. Clatter from heavy steel wheels and electric switches were enhanced, people stood on concrete platforms awaiting trains. Harsh clamor erupted as a metal serpent entered the station. A train came to a stop, the doors automatically retracted. Commuters entered and exited the car simultaneously. The enclosure was overfilled, passengers stood holding onto poles and straps for balance while others sat. The group observed passengers reading newspapers and listening to electronic devices. Damian noticed everyone seemed preoccupied; no one communicated much with one another. The group watched lights zip by in the darkened tunnel. The guys exited the train at another unfamiliar setting, but drew comfort in seeing the area was predominantly African-Americans.

"Where are we going?" asked Dexter. He glanced around puzzled.

"Let's walk, we'll find something," stated Chuck. He seemed more calm and in control of his emotions than the others.

"We're almost broke. I suggest we think of something fast," stated Stan. "Besides, I'm hungry."

They came across a huge street with three lanes of traffic moving in both directions. Vehicles traveled quickly upon the roadway. They crossed the massive roadway to see a colossal brick structure loomed ahead with a huge stone sign overhead. People single-filed into the building. A man was passing.

"Excuse me sir. Can you tell me what is this place?" asked Damian.

The stranger's appearance was disheveled with soiled oversized clothing and matted hair. He eyed Damian and the group strangely, finding the question odd. "That's a shelter, a place where you can get a free meal and bed for the night. They're serving clam chowder soup and sandwiches. If you're going in you'll have to act fast because there's only so many beds available."

"Thank you." They watched the man hurry along toward the shelter.

"Well? What do you think guys?" asked Dexter.

"I say we go for it. What have we to lose?" retorted Stan.

"He's right! It'll save us some cash until we can figure out what to do next," agreed Chuck.

"We need time to plan our next move. Honestly speaking, I feel something out of our control happened to us back in Detroit. It's the only explanation for our actions. None of us are murders, the strange thing is we did it simultaneously. We need to focus and address the issue," stated Rufus.

"Okay, that settles it. We're going inside. Remember, stay close to one another," instructed Damian.

32.

Cheryl awaken abruptly from a profound vivid dream; perspiration dotted her forehead. She walked into the living room to see Zesty sound asleep on the couch. Gently, she tapped her shoulder.

Zesty stirred and opened her eyes. "What is it? Is everything all right?" Her voice was groggy as she sat up and wiped sleep from her eyes.

"I don't know how to explain it, but I think we should get out of here now. I have a strange inkling something is about to happen. Please, let's get going."

Zesty's voice was hoarse. "To where?"

Cheryl shrugged her shoulders. "I don't know, let's just go."

***

Detective Byrd acted quickly with the information he received from Delroy. He experienced an inclination that Zesty was not forthright with her explanation; her story didn't add up. He'd checked her background and discovered no prior felonies. Cheryl and her were squeaky clean. *Hmm…it just doesn't make sense.* The only break he received was from the forensic laboratory, they analyzed a blood sample discovered at the scene belonging to Zesty. *So you were there. Why the cover-up?* His first stop was to visit Zesty's apartment. Surprisingly, he found it unoccupied. He stood on the porch and peered into the house through a window. The detective rubbed his chin absentmindedly when he was in contemplation mode. *You girls can run, but you can't hide forever.* Inside the unmarked sedan, Detective Byrd contacted the dispatcher, his voice resonated in the confined space of the vehicle. "I want an all-point-bulletin placed on the vehicle belonging to Cheryl Hollander. She lives on 123 Shermont Road. Also, check Zesty's address and files for proper identification."

***

"Where are we going?"

Cheryl kept her eyes on the road. "Far away from this place." She drove onto a wooded area and stopped at a specific location. Cheryl exited the vehicle and removed a shovel from the trunk. She walked ten paces and began digging. Curiosity controlled Zesty's mind as she exited the vehicle and neared Cheryl who worked frantically to unearth something. Cheryl exhumed an item covered with plastic from the cold ground. The parcel was duct taped and layered in more plastic. She wiped dirt from the package. At first glance, Zesty thought the parcel was related to drugs. She continued to watch quietly as Cheryl removed plastic layers from the package until she reached the core. A leather tote bag bulged from the contents within. She glanced at Zesty. "Come on."

They returned to the vehicle and drove onward. The two rode in silence for a few miles; both were lost in thoughts. Zesty broke the silence.

"What's in the bag Cheryl?"

Cheryl smiled and took her eyes from the roadway for a moment. "That my friend is my rainy day umbrella. Today it's raining." Her eyes returned to the road. "Everyone in our profession need to have one. I'm surprised you didn't. You know we can't dance forever. Gravity will not allow our bodies to hold up, you have to prepare for the inevitable." Zesty didn't respond. She knew the statement was true. "We'll have to ditch this car soon."

"How did you know it was time to leave?"

"I felt a strong premonition, and I didn't question it."

***

After abandoning the vehicle, the ladies boarded a Greyhound bus heading to New York City. Time ceased to exist for Zesty; day turned into night like a blur. She stared out a window at the night sky and artificial lighting on the roadway. Emotionally, she was confused and scared. *What have I done? What did I get my best friend involved in? She doesn't deserve this.*

Cheryl sat in the aisle seat next to Zesty sensing her friend's uneasiness. "Don't sit there worrying, everything is gonna be all right. We have enough money until we can figure things out."

Zesty gazed at Cheryl through teary eyes. "I'm sorry for getting you into this. When we get to New York, I'll turn myself in."

"You'll what?" interjected Cheryl. Her voice rose. "You'll do no such thing! What will you say? You killed a man and I helped you do it?"

"Of course not, I would never do anything to hurt you. You are all I have." The dams in her eye ducts collapsed as tears cascaded down her cheeks. "I love you."

Caught in compassion and emotional turmoil, Cheryl also began tearing. "I love you too." The moment was heartfelt as they embraced.

33.

"Wow! This place is amazing. Who own it?"

Dr Baden smiled. "I do. Actually, the golfing organization I belong to owns the land. Each member is allotted a place to stay whenever they feel the need to play. It's also a great place to socialize during tournament season. Come on, let's go inside. I know you're hungry and tired."

"Yes, in that order."

A bi-level Victorian structure loomed ahead. Painted shutters and sashes decorated the exterior. Spiral bannisters were noted as she entered. The interior was elegantly designed with antiquated furnishings. Dr Baden gave Genesis a grand tour of the entire house. The journey ended in the den. Genesis flopped on a sofa totally exhausted from the entire ordeal.

"I'll fix us something to eat. There's clothing in the room that should fit you. You'll also find a bathroom you can use to clean up and change. I'll call you when dinner is ready."

"Thank you."

Genesis felt rejuvenated after the shower. Distinctive aroma filled the air. Delightful scents from sautéed garlic, onions, peppers, and baked bread were irresistible. Genesis followed the scent into a well designed kitchen with stainless-steel appliances. A wall mounted oven and refrigerator decorated the kitchen. A marble countertop island was erected in the center of the room. Copper pots hung overhead from brass hooks. Wooden stools were placed around the countertop.

"The food is ready, have a seat." The setting was impressive. Silence overshadowed the room for a few minutes. Dr Baden and Genesis were busy savoring and devouring the meal.

Genesis broke the silence. "Where did you learn to cook like this?" She dabbed the corners of her mouth with a napkin.

"I used to be married. My wife cooked and I helped. I guess it rubbed off on me."

"That's a good thing." Genesis placed more food into her mouth. "Where is she now?" She watched his expression change.

Dr Baden placed his fork on the plate. "She died in an automobile accident three years ago." The subject was still painful for him to speak about.

"I am so sorry. I had no idea."

Dr Baden held up a hand. "Nonsense! You had no way of knowing. They were in an all-girl reunion." He gestured with air quotes. "My daughter Sherry was texting me while driving when the accident happened." His voice trailed off as grief returned.

"I'm so sorry. Is that why you have clothes that fit me here?"

He nodded his head. "You and her were about the same size and height. To be honest, you remind me a lot of Sherry. I guess that's one of the reasons I couldn't stand to see you carted off to some prison."

Genesis reached over and touched his hand. "Please believe, I am not a killer."

"Yes, there's no question in my mind. With the amount of thandiasine in your bloodstream, there's no way you are responsible for your actions. The question is how is it being controlled? Why would anyone want to do this?" He stood. "I'm going to find out who's behind this. Tomorrow we visit an Urban Ink World shop. After that we go to the media. If it's as big as I think, we'll need the security of the press on our side."

***

Detective Walters sat behind a desk conversing on the telephone. His assistant entered as he placed the receiver on the cradle.

"Marge, I need for you to research a chemical referred to as thandiasine. I want all the information you can find on something called i-Ink. Call in a few favors if you must."

"Yes sir." She turned and exited the office.

Detective Walters studied the information in front of him. A notion came to mind; he pressed the intercom button on his desk. "Marge, I want you to see what you can find on a Dr Baden. He's employed at King's County Medical Center."

34.

The shelter was at full capacity. After being assigned beds for the evening, the group stood in a lengthy line to received a free meal. Damian and the guys remained close by one another. The meals were nothing like at home but they were nutritious. The group realized it was an intelligent money-saving decision. The experience was uncanny; never had they ventured so far away from home. After the meals, the guys visited a recreation room. Men sat around tables conversing; some played table top games. A large screen television held an audience. A local news channel broadcasted a breaking news flash. A daring escape from a hospital was plastered on the screen. The group listened.

...that's because it's said the two are now at large. There are no other informative leads at the moment. The authorities believe Dr Baden may be held against his will. Conflicting testimonies suggest Dr Baden may be involved aiding in the

prisoner's escape. The result of the daring escapade left a police officer dead. This is Karen Proctor for Channel 7 Eyewitness News…

"Wow! That's crazy! They ain't kidding when they say this town is tough," remarked Stan.

Another headline news story followed. *"…just in. A simple game of basketball in a local recreation center in Detroit turned into a series of murders. A gangland competition against rivals turned sour. The footage is fuzzy because it was videotaped by an amateur with the used of a cellphone. You can see what looks like a prearranged plot against their rivals. A group of five struck simultaneously, killing the rival team members. You can see the culprits making a dash for the door, and blending in with the other frantic bystanders. The young men have been identified as…"*

"Come on, let's get outta here," whispered Damian. Rufus and Chuck couldn't believe what they witnessed. They continued staring at the screen in disbelief. The group viewed it as an out-of-body experience. Dexter dislodged Chuck and Rufus from their reverie by touching them on the shoulder. The guys eased from room and headed toward the corridor. They moved stealthily through a side emergency exit.

The temperature outside had declined. Shivers consumed most of the guys as they were not accustom to the drastic climate change. The scanty clothing worn was ill-suited for New York's temperatures. The group stood at a corner near a high volume traffic area.

"What now?" asked Chuck. He gazed at the unfamiliar surroundings. The guys went into a huddle.

"I think we should keep moving. We don't know if someone inside the shelter noticed us. Maybe they'll turn us in for a fast buck.

Everyone in there seemed down on their luck," retorted Stan.

"We can't just stand here," said Dexter. The group headed aimlessly down a block.

***

Kenny Washington made arrangements to get a flight to Goshen, a small town located in Orange County. It was the closest town with an airport. Newburgh township is the place where his vehicle is impounded which brought confusion as to how his vehicle arrived at the location. Feelings of guilt and regret emerged deep from within; Kenny felt remorse and sadness because of the way he treated Damian. *I hope he's safe and sound. I've got to find him.* An afterthought arose. *Then I'm gonna kill him for all the trouble he has caused his mom.* The thought brought about a smile. The plane landed safely. Kenny took a taxicab to the town of Newburgh.

Entering the precinct, Kenny was surprised at the level of law enforcement activity for a township of that size. He approached the desk sergeant. "My name is Kenny Washington, I'm here to reclaim my vehicle. I reported it stolen and was told to come here to identify it."

"Please have a seat and someone will be with you momentarily."

Kenny took a seat on a hard wooden bench, he busied himself by watching the activity in the room. Defendants were handcuffed and escorted to different locations. The sound of chains amplified in the setting. A plain-clothed detective approached Kenny with an outstretched hand.

"I'm sorry for keeping you waiting. As you can see it's very busy. My name is Detective Olsen. Please follow me." The detective led Kenny down two flights of stairs and through a steel door. They approached the sports utility vehicle. "Is this your vehicle?"

Kenny gave the vehicle a quick glance. "Yes."

"Lucky for you the vehicle had tracking. Otherwise, this would have been stripped to the bone like a turkey on Thanksgiving day. We caught the thieves redhanded. The plates are from Detroit. How do you reckon it got this far? The thugs we caught inside the vehicle couldn't have driven it from there; they're local hoods."

"I was thinking maybe my son…" Kenny hesitated. He didn't want to give Damian's name because he didn't know if the news about him had reached there. "Actually, my stepson. His name is Curtis. I'm worried about him because he was to be traveling with five of his teammates."

"I'm sorry we have no information about the matter."

"Would it be possible to question the guys in hopes of finding the whereabouts of my son and his friends?"

The detective scratched his chin. "That's a highly irregular request. I'll have to ask my superior. In the meantime, let's get this vehicle situation squared away."

***

The group walked down a quiet side street with connected houses. The designs were similar, the only variation were the color schemes of the stone exteriors. As the group reached the middle of the block, noise resonated from ahead. The source of the commotion was unknown. Curiosity overwhelmed the group as they continued onward. Cars were parked on both sides of the residential street. A few feet ahead, the source of the noise became evident. Between two parked vehicles, a girl was in distress. The woman was being molested. Damian was the first to react. The attacker reached for a young woman as she plead for help. Damian grasped the guy from behind and snatched him away from the girl.

The attacker was taken by surprise. "Hey! What the..?"

The aggressor was much bigger and stronger. He broke free from Damian's grasp. Dexter charged at him forcefully. The momentum sent the two crashing onto a parked car. A loud thud erupted on the quiet block. Stan and Chuck teamed together and began pounding on the giant. Powerful punches rained upon the predator's body and face. Damian regain his clasp on the arms of the aggressor from behind, restricting his movement. The force from the blows rendered him unconscious. Damian hurried to the aid of the woman. They gazed into one another's eyes. She trembled from the natural elements and fear. He noticed her beauty immediately and was impressed. Damian helped her to stand. She was approximately five feet seven inches tall, curly jet-black hair, and noticeable flawless features. The lady wore a denim skirt along and a leather jacket. The short-length skirt exposed bruises on her knees. She placed her hands in Damian's allowing him to assist her to stand. Damian felt the softness of her skin and the warmth of her touch. The guys stood guard over the attacker in the event he revived. The woman sobbed as she dabbed at her bruised legs. She brushed her soiled clothing with her hands as self-consciousness invaded her perception.

"Thank you all, it was a brave thing you did. You're not from around here because nobody helps in these parts. They're afraid of the reprisals from the thugs."

"Do you have far to go? We can walk you the rest of the way if you'd like."

"I have a distance to travel, but I wasn't walking." She pointed to her vehicle. "He attacked me as I was making my way to the car. Please get in. I'll take you guys anywhere you'd like." The guys gazed at one another. Each felt a pleasant vibe as they entered the vehicle.

"My name is Damian. This here is Stan, Chuck, Rufus, and Dexter." Damian sat in the front passenger seat.

"I am so thankful. I don't know what would have happened if you hadn't came along. I was visiting a girlfriend who happened to not be home. I've pleaded with her to move out of that neighborhood. The guy came out of nowhere and attacked me. He was strong and I couldn't break free." Tears cascaded down her cheeks as she recalled the horrific incident.

"It's all right now. You're safe."

She glanced at Damian and smiled. "My name is Faith Sampson." Her eyes returned to the roadway. "How can I ever repay you guys? Where do you want to go?"

The guys in the rear remained quiet. "We're from Detroit," stated Damian.

"Detroit? That explains it," retorted Faith. "What are you doing in New York?"

"It's a long story. I can say we ran into bad luck ourselves, we have no place to go." Damian's voice was a whisper.

"Where were you headed?"

"It was suppose to be a short trip, but my dad's vehicle was stolen. Here we are."

"That is so sad." Silence filled the confine space. Faith felt a safe vibe from the group. *Normally, I would never say or do what I'm about to. I feel it's the right thing to do,* she contemplated. "I'll tell you what. It's Friday evening, you can stay at my house for the weekend. Don't get any ideas, because I never would consider doing something like this for strangers. Since you guys went out on the limb for me, it's the least I can do to help."

Appreciation in the form of thanks came from the rear. "Faith that's very nice of you. You don't owe us anything. We would have done that for anyone," said Damian.

"I feel like it." Her smile lingered toward Damian.

35

PORT OF AUTHORITY/BUS TERMINAL
NEW YORK CITY

Zesty and Cheryl exited the massive terminal onto a neon-lit metropolis. The city was alive with energy; people and vehicles moved about the streets. Restaurants and theaters were busy.

"Where're we going?" asked Zesty.

"Let's find a place to rest. Afterward, we can figure out our next move. We'll get some take-out and eat in the room."

They continued along 7th Avenue. "I've been here on a field trip with the school. We visited the Jacob Javis Center, and the prices in the area were high. We traveled to Brooklyn because the cost was reasonable. Come on, I know the way."

Zesty and Cheryl exited the subway to another unfamiliar territory. The area was less busy compared to Manhattan. An active intersection loomed ahead; the sounds of traffic filled the air. Excited partygoers crowded a doorway of a storefront lounge. A sign overhead read Club Oasis. Cheryl stared ahead as if mesmerized. What captured her attention was a window ad. A help wanted sign was posted specifing immediate hire.

"I know you're not thinking what I think you're thinking." Zesty's demeanor was stern.

Cheryl broke her stare and faced Zesty. "Yes, it's perfect! It's something we're both good at. It'll be a good cover. We can do it for a little while and see what happens."

Zesty took a moment to contemplate. "I'll do it! Remember, only for a little while."

Club Oasis held an upscale mature setting. Music played as girls sashayed upon a runway displaying the latest in lingeries designed by local talent. Ladies straddled chrome poles on another stage. Currency of different denominations littered the stage floor. Men and women watched the show.

Cheryl and Zesty applied for the positions and were immediately hired. After finding a take-out restaurant, the women rented a room at a motel for a week.

***

Detective Byrd sat behind his desk reviewing the forensic data from the crime scene where Stax was found dead. The detective worked diligently to uncover the link between Zesty, Cheryl, and Stax. Frustration from not knowing took a toll; a pencil he held snapped in two parts involuntarily just as the telephone rang. Detective Byrd snatched up the receiver. "Homicide Division, this is Detective Byrd.

How may I help you?"

"Detective Byrd, I'm Detective Walters from New York. We are not acquainted. Somehow our investigations are now entangled. We are working on a case here and noticed a strange pattern of violence happening in different parts of the country. Two which were in your area. Both incidents are in the Detroit area. A group of five boys playing basketball suddenly turned violent. The members from the opposing team were killed. Another bizarre incident is a dancer we think murdered a man."

Detective Byrd was now intrigued by the caller's knowledge. "How do you know about that? How are these things related?"

Detective Walters realized he commanded the detective's full attention. "For beginners, the subjects committed crimes on the same day, and in close proximity."

"I still don't understand." He was given an abridged version of the story. Detective Byrd was invited to join in on the investigation with Detective Walters in New York. The direct details were too sensitive to speak about on the telephone.

36.

Genesis and Dr Baden entered one of the many Urban Ink World tattoo parlors in the region. Being midday, the parlor wasn't busy. A few booths held customers where mechanical buzz resonated from tattoo guns. The ambiance in the parlor was mellow, soft music played from overhead ceiling speakers. The reception clerk sat reading a magazine behind a station.

Genesis approached. "I have a design I would like to have tattooed on my right thigh."

The clerk, a young man of Puerto Rican descent, stood to greet Genesis. He studied her curvaceous figure and pretty face as he approached from around the counter. *Wow! She's definitely a ten.* He smiled. "Can I see it?" Genesis handed him the design. It was a technical drawing of symmetric lines intertwined. She created the design last night while at Dr Baden's golf home. She tried to design it as complex as possible so it would be almost impossible to recreate. "Wow! It is something. Let's see if we have similar designs." Genesis followed him to a display wall located at the rear of the shop. The place was slightly out of view from the front.

Dr Baden feigned interested in a design. As soon as he saw Genesis lead the clerk away from the station, he went into action. The doctor eased behind the clerk's desk and sat. He gained access into the computer with ease. Genesis taught him an unorthodox shortcut into the world of hacking. Dr Baden was able to maneuver the information he desired. Keying in the word i-Ink amazed him. His eyes grew wide from excitement. He was intrigued to find the information he sought was tied to the United States Department of Defense. The doctor logged out of the computer and eased away from the area. At that moment, Genesis steered the clerk toward the front. The task for her was easy because the clerk was mesmerized with her body. She smiled. *Typical male.* With the information memorized, Dr Baden exited the premises. He waited near the corner for Genesis to arrive. She approached him with a confident smile.

"I thought I would have to get a restraining order for him," she giggled.

Dr Baden smiled. "You can't blame him for having excellent taste."

Genesis blushed; her cheeks became rosy red. "Are you flirting with me?" Dr Baden held up his hands defensively and continued to smiled. Before he could answer, Genesis responded for him. "I like it. Now what did you find out?"

"This rabbit hole is deeper than any of us could have imagined. Come on, let's walk." Dr Baden glanced at the surroundings feeling unnerved. He flagged a taxicab.

"The link has technical jargon. I was able to ascertain the ink has a neurological property with a chemical base element being thandiasine."

"That explains the chemical you've discovered in my body. Can't you get it out of me?"

"I've done some research, and discovered if the element is extracted too urgently, it could kill the host. It seems that i-Ink is a messenger serum that works on the organs and nerve system. It causes violent outburst by use of a high frequency. My wonder is what would the defense department want with such an element? Why push it upon unsuspecting American citizens through ink parlors? What would that accomplish?"

"So you're saying I am being used remotely?"

He nodded. "Yes, there are more subjects other than yourself this experiment is being used on. The subjects are throughout the country. For a substance of this nature to work it would have to be done discretely. In order to accomplish it, they must use unsuspecting subjects. All we have to do now is match the day of your outbreak to others on that very same day."

"Where are we going to find that kind of data? You said so yourself we are dealing with the defense department." Genesis was perplexed.

Dr Baden tapped on the plexiglass partition to gain the driver's attention. "Driver, take us to the New York Times building." Dr Baden faced Genesis. "There's more, I hacked into a highly classified clearance program. They'll be coming after us and whomever has anything to do with the interference."

"Can I use your cellphone?" asked Genesis.

"Sure, who are you calling?"

"I have a friend. We attend the same school. Actually she's older, she graduated two years ago. When I don't call, she goes crazy with worry. I don't want her inquiring about me and get jammed." Genesis began dialing.

***

Damian and the guys awoke in a guest room. Delightful aromas of eggs, bacon, toast, and coffee wafted through the air. They made their way downstairs to an unoccupied kitchen. Five steaming plates of food were placed on the table.

"Hmm…" Chuck was impressed. "This is amazing." Everyone sat.

"Wow! This food is fit for a king," said Dexter. His mouth was filled. The sounds of fine chinaware and utensils resonated in the room. An abundance of cheeses and juices were on display. Fresh cut flowers added to the festive ambiance. The guys ate ravenously.

"Maybe we should go into the business of helping damsels in distress," retorted Stan jokingly.

"I wonder where's Faith?" asked Damian. Undeniably, he felt something for her. He sipped orange juice and tossed a napkin onto his plate. He exited the room through a door on the right. Damian was impressed with the size and decor of the house. Imported vases were on stands, and oil paintings adorned walls. Damian found himself walking on smooth concrete tiles. The path led to an in-ground pool area. Faith was in the water swimming laps, her hair covered in a green rubber cap. Her strokes in the water were smooth and fluid. She stopped when Damian approached, and swam toward him.

"Good morning my knight in shining armor." She straddled one of the rungs on the pool ladder and held one hand on the rail. The other hand was outstretched toward Damian. He gently assisted her from the water.

"Thank you." Damian reached for a beach towel from a deck chair and wrapped her with it. He used the opportunity to observe her beautiful contours. "Did you find enough to eat?"

"Yes, it was delicious."

The two sat across from one another; each in their own thought. Faith continuously dabbed at her damp body with the towel. Damian noticed her eyes.

"You live here alone? You must be an entertainer."

"I wish." She giggled. "No, this is my parent's house. They're away for the weekend. That's why you're here." Damian studied the massive pool. "Would you like to go for a swim?" The rest of the guys appeared. Faith's attention was adverted toward them. "I was just inviting Damian here to swim. Would you guys like to join in?"

"Sure."

"Yeah!"

"You bet!"

"Yeah!" The excited responses were said in unison.

"Okay, in the guest room where you guys slept you will find swim trunks of many sizes in the closet. Help yourself." The guys hurried to change. Damian lingered behind. Faith gazed into his eyes. "My father owns a department store."

The guys emerged shirtless, and wearing colorful swim trunks. Faith noticed their identical tattoos.

"What's the significance of the tattoos?" She was intrigued by the designs. The others jumped into the water creating huge splashes.

Damian gazed at his tattoo. "We're real tight with one another. We're not a gang, if that's what you are insinuating."

"Did I say that?"

"Back home we are on the varsity team, and we beat the rival school for state championship. We went out to celebrate, and returned with these to show our brotherhood. It was all impromptu."

"I like that. It's special."

"Faith there's something I would like to share with you."

"Can't it wait?" Surprisingly, she pushed Damian into the pool and dove in afterward.

The group spent an abundant amount of time in the water. They chose two teams and played volleyball. Laughter and excitement filled the air. Tiredness and hunger overwhelmed the group afterward. Faith cooked a hearty lunch of fillet chicken breast, rice, and salad. Everyone felt content afterward. She invited them to watch a movie in a room that held a giant screen and comfortable recliner chairs. A high vaulted ceiling gave the room a commercial theatrical atmosphere. An electric popcorn machine was stationed near a door. The group ended the afternoon conversing in the living room. They became bonded in spirit. Faith really like the guys, and held a special liking for Damian. Her cellphone rang; she studied the display on the screen and turned toward the group. "Will you excuse me while I take this call?"

"Sure, go right ahead," replied Damian.

Faith exited the room and spoke in a low tone. "Where the hell are you? Do you know I got mugged on a visit to your house? Right on your block." From that moment forward, Faith listened to Genesis explained her plight. She interrupted occasionally. "Carlos is dead?" She continued listening as tears swelled in the corners of her eyes. Genesis explained all she could about the tattoo and Urban Ink World. She told her about Dr Baden and how he risked his job and life to save her. Faith was too distraught to talk about the guys she met.

"I wanted you to hear it from me before you watched it on the news. I promise you I'll straighten things out." The line was disconnected.

Faith studied the cellphone as if she held a foreign object. The news was upsetting. Trembling, she headed back into the room to join the others.

Damian was the first to notice her changed demeanor. He hurried to her aid. "Faith! What's wrong?" He led her to a couch.

Chuck hurried toward the kitchen, and returned with a glass of water. He handed her the glass.

Faith sipped on the cool liquid. "Please, turn on the television." She explained some of what was told to her. A local newscast conveyed the story about Genesis. A photograph posted her as a cop killer. A manhunt was underway for her capture, along with a reward of twenty thousand dollars for any information leading to an arrest.

A notion struck. Faith looked toward the guys standing around her with concerned expressions. She remembered what Genesis said about the tattoos and Urban Ink World. "Can I ask you something?"

"Sure anything," replied Stan.

"Yeah go ahead," said Damian.

"Where did you guys get those tattoos? And when?"

Damian answered. "A few days ago. We got them done at Urban Ink World." He watched her facial expression. "Why do you ask? What is it?"

"My friend had a tattoo done there also. They offered her a free one."

"So did we," interjected Dexter. He displayed his complimentary tattoo.

"She said the tattoo caused her to do something evil. She couldn't explain how." Faith pointed to the television screen. "That's my friend they're talking about. I am telling you she isn't the type of person who would do something like that." The dams in the corner of her eyes collapsed. The guys felt an eerie sensation as they glanced at one another for recognition.

Damian explained. "There's something I was trying to tell you earlier. We too were offered the same appreciative package. You see?" Damian displayed his tattoo. He sighed deeply as he realized he was at the point of no return. Damian explained the entire plight starting with the tattoo to the basketball game and the reason they were in New York.

Faith sat confused and exhausted. She was emotionally split between being afraid and wanting to help the guys that saved her life.

155

"Okay, we'll figure this thing out together."

37.

Kenny Washington sat outside the interrogation room peering through a one-way glass partition. His request to question the defendant was denied. Instead, he was compensated another way. Kenny was allowed to watch the ongoing proceeding. Inside the interrogation room, Detective Byrd's large frame loomed over Delroy. What was being said wasn't audible to Kenny, but he studied Delroy's body language and concluded the right questions weren't being asked. A detective approached. "Why can't I ask just one question?" asked Kenny feeling agitated.

"I told you Mr Washington, it would taint the case if it were to go to trial." He shook his head. "No can do."

Kenny eagerly approached Detective Byrd as he exited the interrogation room. "Did he tell you anything useful?"

Detective Byrd shook his head. "I'm really sorry. He said they took the truck without knowing who it belonged to."

"What is his legal name?"

The unorthodox question caught Detective Byrd off guard. "Delroy Taylor. Why?"

"I just wanted to know the name of the person that stole my vehicle. I feel I deserve to know who caused me all this wasted time. Thank you for your help gentlemen." Kenny headed toward the exit. The two detectives were left standing.

"I've got a funny feeling about this one," stated Detective Byrd. He watched as Kenny Washington exited the room.

***

A block from the precinct, Kenny Washington entered a storefront office. A bail bondsmen sign was above the door. Kenny entered to find a man sitting behind a document-littered desk. The unkempt office was unoccupied. The man stood with an outstretched hand. Kenny immediately sized him up. Black hair, pockmarked skin, slender nose, slight mustache, and a connecting goatee. He also observed the man was approximately five feet six inches, slightly overweight, and he wore a tieless button-up shirt. The bondsman suit jacket hung on the back of a chair. Exposed was a leather holster that housed a semi-automatic handgun. The two shook hands.

"My name is Dave Colter. What can I do for you?" He gestured for Kenny to sit.

"My name is Kenny Washington. My sister's silly son has been arrested for auto theft of my vehicle. He's in the county jail. I feel he's learned his lesson and I want to bail him out."

"Okay, what's his name?"

"Delroy Taylor."

The bail bondsman began typing in the information into his computer. He read the data from the screen. The monitor was out of Kenny's line of vision. "It says here your nephew has been busy over the years. His bond is seventy five hundred dollars. Ten percent of that comes out to seven hundred fifty dollars cash."

"Excellent." Kenny retrieved his wallet.

"Please fill out this form."

***

Delroy Taylor exited the county jail tired and hungry. His appearance was disheveled; his hair and clothing were in disarray. In all of his years of doing petty crimes, Delroy never made bail. *Who could have sprung me?* He looked around with uncertainty, and saw not one familiar face. No one paid him any attention as people moved about on the street. As he reached the bottom of the steps, a voice called out his name. The sound came from behind.

"Delroy! Delroy Taylor!"

Delroy stopped. He felt goose bumps develop on his arms. A chill ran up his spine. He turned around to see a complete stranger standing near what looked like the vehicle he was arrested for stealing.

Kenny approached him. "I just need a minute of your time."

Delroy eyed the man skeptically, he thought the man wanted to retaliate for taking his vehicle. "I don't know you."

"Correct, but I know you. I'm the one that bailed your sorry-ass out of jail."

Delroy glanced toward the vehicle then returned his attention to Kenny. "What do you want?"

"Get in the vehicle."

Delroy became dismayed at the request. He wanted to turn and bolt down the street, but two emotions discouraged the actions. He was afraid of the unknown and he was inquisitive to know what was going on. "Look man, I'm sorry about your vehicle."

"That's not what I'm concerned about." Kenny gestured with a hand for him to enter the vehicle.

Feeling intimidated, Delroy entered the vehicle. They drove pass the main street and headed toward the interstate. Nervousness permeated Delroy's being.

"Where are we going?"

"Listen, there were five boys inside this vehicle when you jacked it. Where are they?"

"Yes, there were five guys. I thought they were a new crew coming into town to take over the drug trade. Just like the Jamaicans did last month. We saw the out-of-town plates so we jacked them for it. It was only when they went into the motel on State Street. We didn't get too far because the damn thing shut off."

"What happened to the five guys?"

"I told you they were in the motel. Word on the street was they caught a Greyhound bus on 27th Street. That bus only goes to New York City. That's an hour and a half ride from here."

Kenny stopped the vehicle. "Get out!" His voice was stern. "Find yourself another profession."

Delroy studied Kenny's demeanor. For a moment he thought the man might shoot him in the back when he exited the vehicle. Delroy hesitantly obeyed the request. Kenny placed the vehicle in gear and continued onward. His destination was New York City.

38.

UNITED STATES DEPARTMENT OF DEFENSE
CONFERENCE ROOM
WASHINGTON, DISTRICT OF COLUMBIA

Four highly decorated uniformed men, each representing a different branch of the armed forces, were seated around a rectangular conference table. In attendance was Lieutenant Satchel. The lieutenant's field data encouraged a favorable decision from the group. The initial test of Project i-Ink was officially used on foreign soil. Afghanistan was the targeted country because of its concentrated employment of Taliban soldiers. Most of the soldiers were poor and were being paid small fees to carry out orders for the regime. The money meant their families would survive the cold winters in the barren mountainous region. Others were forced into the organization from fear of harm to their families. The first intelligence report was a success, the men were proud with the project. Lieutenant Satchel was given consideration for his role.

"Lieutenant Satchel, I want to be one of the first to congratulate you on your successful research with Project i-Ink. Without your participation and insight, the project wouldn't have progressed so quickly. The franchises of ink parlors is a perfect cover. In a couple of weeks, when the first field test results are due, you should be expecting a promotion with our recommendations." He gestured to the others sitting around the table. General Major Weatherby, an executive officer for the Army, was happy to make the announcement.

"Thank you sir."

The men stood and shook hands; the meeting was concluded. A clerk approached the lieutenant as he walked along the corridor with other officials.

"Sir, there's a message for you." The clerk handed the lieutenant a note and walked away.

Lieutenant Satchel read the message. "Excuse me gentlemen duty calls."

"Go right ahead." The high ranking officers watched the lieutenant head down the corridor.

Lieutenant Satchel made a call that was answered on the second ring. "What do you have?" The lieutenant listened attentively to the voice on the other end. The call was terminated shortly thereafter. He dialed another number and gave instructions to a recipient before disconnecting the call. The lieutenant entered a military-issued vehicle and drove to an awaiting aircraft on an airstrip. He was bound for

Great Falls, Montana. He stared out the window at the clear blue sky and reflected on the data recorded on his laptop. His mind wondered about the test subjects that were exposed on United States soil. *It's time to end all the interference once and for all. I'm almost where I want to be, I don't intend to let anyone get in my way.* The thought brought a smile.

***

Detective Byrd received a police escort from the airport. Within the hour, he sat face to face with Detective Walters.

"Detective Byrd, I'm happy you could make it on such short notice."

"I'm still on the clock. I just hope this doesn't waste the taxpayer's money."

"I think not. A certain death led us to investigate a substance. The base chemical in this neuron agent is highly restricted in the United States. The finished product from this plant is called thandiasine. The substance comes only from one location in the world, and that's South America. This is where things gets interesting. Thousands of pounds of this stuff was shipped to a manufacturing plant in Great Falls, Montana. This place manufacture inks."

"If the substance is illegal in the United States how did it clear customs?"

"That's where it gets weird. It was authorized and escorted in by the Department of Defense."

"What does that have to do with me?"

"That manufacturing plant is contracted out to a franchise called

Urban Ink World. The tattoo parlors have sprung up all over the country. I think a pattern is developing. A week ago there were series of violent crimes. Our computer network capabilities, thanks to 911, was able to access the information to see what was going on in every part of the country. Here in New York, we're looking for a young girl with no criminal record whatsoever. Her boyfriend died saving the life of a little boy. Drugs were found in her residence, but I'm sure she's innocent. Anyway, she became spooked and ended up killing a police officer. Five youths kill another group during an innocent game of basketball in your city. It was caught on tape. Then, there's a burnt victim. What I am saying is the comparisons are very similar; each wore similar tattoos."

Detective Byrd stood and began pacing. "Are you suggesting some kind of conspiracy is taking place? You think the government is involved?"

"I don't know what to think at this point. I'm just stating facts. Since you're here let's find out."

39.

Zesty and Cheryl had been dancing on stage for a week. The clientele was upscale and the money was lucrative compared to the earnings they received in Detroit. The two were in a motel room relaxing.

"Girl with the kind of cash we're pulling in, we should think twice about leaving. I know now why people say the Big Apple is the place to be."

Zesty was concerned. "Don't forget the cops are on our trail."

"Whatever!" retorted Cheryl. She took a sip of wine. "I'm going to do a gig. One thousand dollars for a two hour private dance session. This will help us tremendously."

"Cheryl I don't like it! We've just arrived. Don't it make you wonder why he didn't ask the other girls? Why you so suddenly?"

The wine took effect on Cheryl; intoxication caused her to giggle.

"Maybe he's tired of the old stuff." She dance joyfully around the room. "Maybe he see something better." Her words became slurred.

"If you won't change your mind, then tell me the address to where you'll be staying."

"You're beginning to sound like my mother. I'll be in room 209 at the Galaxy Motel. Just me and Larry. You see those C-notes he tips me with." Cheryl approached a vanity table and began to prep her face. She wore a form-fitted leather outfit that left nothing to the imagination.

Zesty jotted the information. "That means you dance from 12 am to 2 am. You should be back in this room by 2:30 am. Right?" Cheryl didn't respond. "Right?"

"Right."

***

Cheryl knocked on door 209. She heard movement on the other side. The door opened to a tall and dark complexion man. He wore slacks with a button-up shirt. A smile was plastered on his face as he stood at the threshold. He glanced at his wristwatch.

"Perfect timing, I like that. Come in." He stepped aside allowing Cheryl entry into the room. She noticed the space was cramped. A table filled with foods, wines, and candles were off to the side. Larry closed the door without securing it.

"Let me take your jacket." He was in awe at Cheryl's curvaceous figure and pleasant scent.

"Remember two hours of dancing. Right?"

"Sure."

Cheryl held out her hand to receive payment.

"Oh I see, business first." He chuckled and reached into his pocket withdrawing a wad of cash. He peeled off ten crisp hundred dollar bills and handed them to her.

Cheryl placed the bills in her clutch bag. "Okay." She steered Larry toward the bed and gently shoved him upon it. She stepped back to allow him a good view. In a burlesque manner, Cheryl began undressing. Larry was mesmerized by Cheryl's experience, enticing moves, and became immediately erect. Cheryl wore a designer bra and panty set; the material was satin and lace. Images of cherries covered the crotch and nipple area.

"You like what you see?"

"You know I do. How about we cut to the chase and let's do the damn thang?"

"I told you before this isn't that kind of party."

Larry's smile. "Sure it is." He reached into his pocket and withdrew cash and peeled off more hundred dollar bills. "Now that's two grand. I ain't never met any coochie that expensive." He tossed the cash in the air causing the bills to rained upon her.

Cheryl felt an eerie sensation, but dismissed the emotion and contemplated on making money. Her thoughts changed. "Nah, let's just stick to the plan. I dance for you in the nude nothing more."

"That's cool, give me my money worth." Larry sat up on the bed with his feet touching the floor. He stared at Cheryl as she disrobed. Her pose displayed confidence with her body. *I've gotta have it.* Larry glanced at his wristwatch. *Damn an hour has already gone by.*

Tattoo

Cheryl gyrated to the sound of reggae music. She glanced at Larry as he placed his hand on his crotch; his mouth gaped open.

"Give me the rest of those bills and I'll give you your money worth." She winked slyly.

Larry hurriedly tossed more cash at her feet. "That's right baby give it to me."

Cheryl sashayed to the table and returned with a champagne bottle. She popped open the cork. The content in the bottle ejected forcefully. Clear liquid mixed with compressed gas escaped. Cheryl placed her finger over the opening of the bottle and shook the content. She inserted the bottle neck into her warm and wet orifice. The content of the bottle gushed filling her. A pleasurable moan was audible as the sparkling liquid titillated her senses. She removed the bottle and allowed Larry to drink from the bottle. He did so eagerly.

"You want more juice?"

"You know I do baby." He couldn't control himself any longer as lust heightened within. *I've got to have her.*

"Come, place your mouth here." She gestured toward her opening.

Larry's face was only inches away as Cheryl released champagne on his face and shirt. He didn't seem to mind. As the sexual escapade heightened, Cheryl allowed him to bed her. She was unaware the doorknob to the room slowly turned. The door was now ajar. A man wearing dark jeans, urban boots, and a leather jacket quietly entered the room. Covertly, the intruder eased his way closer to the bed. He wore black leather gloves and a knitted cap.

Cheryl straddled Larry in a domination position. "That's right, don't stop…" She felt a sudden sensation of pain as her hair was yanked. The force pulled her from the bed onto the floor. Cheryl stared into the barrel of a handgun.

"W-what is this?" Cheryl glance at Larry for help, she noticed his smile and realized it was a setup.

The gunman's menacing eye roamed the room. "I'll tell you what this is. This is a fuckin' gun. It's capable of blowing your pretty little head off. It also means this escapade is a freebie."

Larry retrieved her clutch bag and removed the first set of cash he'd given her. He picked the rest of the money from the floor. "This is what I call rain money." He smiled. "I told you I never had no pussy that expensive in my entire life, and still haven't."

"Get on the bed," demanded the gunman. He nudged her with the barrel of the weapon.

Cheryl was terrified, never have she felt so vulnerable in her entire life. Her body trembled as if the temperature was suddenly lowered in the room.

Larry's smile continued; he displayed no compassion. "I'm gonna show you how this is gonna go." He shoved her onto the bed. The gunman held the weapon pointed at her head.

"Please! You don't have to do…"

SMACK!

The sound was sharp; the blow landed hard across her face. The pain was acute, it felt as if a thousand bees stung simultaneously. Cheryl was manhandled onto the bed and held down. The men began having their way with her.

***

Zesty paced in the motel room; a sense of uneasiness enveloped her being. She was against the idea of working at Club Oasis from the beginning. More so, she was against Cheryl going out with one of the clients who was a complete stranger. Zesty thought about everything Cheryl went through for her in Detroit and wanted to show support. She glanced at her wristwatch as anxiety overwhelmed her. Zesty placed on her jacket, picked up her handbag, and headed out of the door. A light mist blanketed the area with a moist sheen. Zesty flagged a passing taxicab.

"Where to Miss?"

"The Galaxy Motel. I'll throw in a tip if you can get me there quickly."

The driver smiled. "Yes ma'am."

Zesty's mind was in turmoil as streets whizzed pass her line of vision. She checked her watch again. Zesty was jolted as the taxicab came to a sudden halt. The stop removed her from her reverie.

"We're here Miss," said the driver. He spoke through a protective plexiglass partition. The statement was said as a badge of honor.

Zesty studied her surroundings before reaching in her bag for a bill. A thought occurred. Zesty retrieved a hundred dollar bill and ripped the currency in two pieces. The driver looked on bewildered. She handed him half the bill. "I'll give you the other half if you wait a few minutes for me to pick up my friend. This is a bad neighborhood and I don't want to be out here alone. Here…" She handed him another bill. It was a ten dollar bill. "This is for the fare if you decide to leave." She placed the bill through the partition and hurried out of the vehicle.

Zesty entered the motel and headed directly for the stairwell. Her mind recanted what Cheryl had said. ...*we'll be at the Galaxy Motel. Room 209.*

One flight up the staircase, Zesty exited onto a carpeted corridor. She glanced at the numbers on the doors and stopped at room 209. Zesty placed her ear to the door and listened. A faint conversation was audible, the sounds of male voices laughing emitted. A harsh noise shattered through the voices. There was no doubt as to who the voice belonged. Quickly, she reached into her handbag and produced a small caliber handgun. She clutched the weapon tightly as adrenaline flowed from her glands into her bloodstream. Zesty turned the doorknob slowly; to her surprise it was unlocked. She sighed in relief. Using the element of surprise, Zesty forcefully opened the door with the weapon pointed. Her eyes widened as she scanned the room. The area was in disarray; a malodor existed. Total surprise and anger overwhelmed her.

Larry had his back toward the door. He was in the doggy-style position penetrating Cheryl while his partner held her down. She was being totally violated. Cheryl's exhausted screams were faint. Both men stopped abruptly when the front door barged open. The gunman was the only one to have a visual on the intruder. He reached for his weapon on a night stand.

PLOP! PLOP! PLOP!

Loud, thunderous claps filled the room with ear-shattering noise. Bright flashes of fire ejected from the weapon's muzzle. It would be all the gunman would ever experience; the projectiles hit him twice in succession. Once in the chest, the other entered his throat. He fell lifeless onto the floor.

Larry was not prepared for the calamity; he was in an orgasmic state of being. As his body fluids released, hot pain entered his back. Thereafter, he ceased to feel anything. His lifeless body fell upon Cheryl. Dead weight pressed against her naked body as she screamed in agony, pain, and exhaustion. The scent of cordite mixed with urine and feces permeated the room.

Zesty rushed to get Larry's naked body off of Cheryl. She never shot anyone and realized there was no time to analyze the situation. She covered her friend's trembling body with a blanket and scrambled to gather all of Cheryl's possessions.

Cheryl was distraught and crying, her brain hadn't processed what had taken place. She stood languid and drained of emotions. Zesty hastily moved about the apartment removing contents from the men's clothing, and quickly wiping everything she figured Cheryl might have came in contact with. Zesty helped Cheryl dress and escorted her outside.

Zesty sighed deeply when she saw the taxicab in the same position from earlier. The two entered the vehicle and drove off in the misty nocturnal setting.

40.

The tall and massive New York Times building loomed over the city. Flocks of tourist visited the award-winning newspaper company from all over the globe. The area was crowded with people. Dr Baden escorted Genesis pass an elevator bank toward a stairwell. They traveled up two flights exiting on the second floor. Doors on both sides of the corridor were equipped with nameplates. People entered and exited the many doors. Dr Baden entered a microfilm room with Genesis in tow.

Dimmed overhead fixtures restricted light to allow optimum viewing. Chrome and vinyl stools were placed in front of each station. Sound absorbing acoustical panels partitioned each station. Dr Baden sat in front of a monitor as Genesis sat next to him. Sound from his fingers moving swiftly upon the keyboard resonated.

"You said this all happened about a week ago. Right?" Genesis responded with a nod. "Okay, let's see what we can find on the United Press International and the American Press International." The screen was split. The monitor displayed different periodicals simultaneously. The doctor cross-matched the dates and story lines. They found Genesis' story. She read it feeling remorse for the slain police officer. Still confused, she didn't remember any details from the incident. No matter how hard she tried to recall the mental images they would not materialize. Genesis was only able to visualize the officer as he lay on the floor after the fact. Her only vivid recollection was the getaway.

Dr Baden noticed her worried expression. "Don't you worry. That wasn't the real you they're talking about." He tapped her shoulder. "Look…" He pointed to another article. "You see? The time frames are close." The caption read FIVE YOUTHS KILL RIVAL TEAM ON B-BALL COURT LITERALLY! They continued reading the article with enthusiasm.

"The picture is grainy. Do you see that?" Genesis pointed to a figure on the screen. "He's wearing a similar tattoo." She excitedly matched it with her own.

"Yes, I see the resemblance." He read another report from the Detroit Press. "It says here a search is in progress for two women in the strange death of a street hustler. Both women have clean records. The incident didn't match any of their profiles. There's no reason why the two disappeared."

Genesis glanced at Dr Baden. "What are we gonna do next?"

"I came here because of the massive research material. I also have a dear friend in this building. We went to school together and parted company when we found our purposes in life. He's now the chief editor here. We're going to his office and tell him our story. We'll use the media as a security blanket to keep us from ending up railroaded. At least until we get our story out in the open. It might give us the leverage needed to stay alive."

"Do you really think it'll work?"

"I honestly don't know. It sure beat the heck out of running for the rest of our lives."

"Can I ask you another question?" Her eyes peered into his.

"Sure, you can ask me anything."

"Why did you come to my aid at the hospital?"

Dr Baden stared into her eyes. "Seeing you for the first time reminded me of my daughter." The thought caused him discomfort. "After hearing your story and investigating it to find you're not a criminal, I felt empathy. When I began running tests and finding what I did, I noticed how the police wanted nothing more than to frame you. Maybe they just wanted to close the case. I couldn't let that happen." He looked away for a moment and found the courage to face her again. "I began feeling a need to protect you, a yearning that intensified over time. I guess it was at that moment I began falling in love with you. Okay, I said it!"

Genesis stared at him as she analyzed what was said. She knew it took courage for him to convey such an emotion verbally. Her facial expression softened. She touched his hand. "I'm glad it happened."

"I know there's an issue with our age difference but..." Genesis quieted him by placing her lips on his. She felt the same emotions, only she didn't know how to express it until now. Dr Baden was taken aback by the gesture. It happened suddenly, and the sensation felt good. The two gazed into one another's eyes. "Come on, let's get the show on the road so we can plan our new life together. That's if you'll have me." Genesis smiled. Dr Baden's cellphone rang, he checked the display to see the caller was using an unregistered number. "Hmm…I wonder who this could be?" He connected with the caller. "Hello?" He listened for a moment and passed the device to Genesis. "It's for you."

Genesis was perplexed. She placed the device to her ear as her expression changed from curiosity to pure delight. Genesis immediately recognized the caller's voice. "Faith! What's going on?" She listened attentively to what was being revealed. Genesis gazed at Dr Baden as she listened. "Okay, we're at the New York Times building on 43rd Street. Bring them here. Okay bye." Genesis handed the cellphone back to Dr Baden. "Things have just gotten bigger and more complicated. It only proves there's a conspiracy ongoing. You remember the five basketball players we read about in Detroit?" Dr Baden nodded in recognition. "Don't ask me how, through twisted fate I guess, the group is at my friend Faith's home. They'll be here soon. Maybe you can continue to do what you've planned. We now have more proof. It will give our story more validity."

The information was a shocker to Dr Baden; the unexpectedness of the news was astounding. The entire probability of it happening seemed surreal. He sensed something dangerous was at play. "I suggest we go to my friend and prep him to the situation before they arrive. This is a lot to take in. We'll need the time to explain."

***

Dr Baden and Genesis sat in the office of the chief editor. Dennis Lexmark, a well-spoken man with salt and pepper hair. He was well-groomed. The doctor hadn't seen his friend in quite some time and was taken aback by Dennis' appearance. The three were seated at a lounge section in his lavish office. A glass table with trade magazines were stacked neatly atop. Dr Baden and Genesis sat on a couch while Mr Lexmark sat behind his desk. After the pleasantries were exhausted, Mr Lexmark listened to the seriousness of the subject matter. He retrieved a tape recorder and a writing pad from his desk.

"You know I would never come here if I were unsure. My own livelihood is at stake."

"I believe you. If the government is involved, we're going to have to get you to a safe house." He reached into his pocket and retrieved a set of keys on a ring. He tossed them to Dr Baden. "Micheal this thing may get nasty. Are you sure you're ready to go all the way with this?"

Dr Baden glanced at Genesis. His attention returned to his friend. "Yes."

"Okay, do you have the toxicology report on Genesis? We'll need the documents on the illegal drug shipments and proof the tattoo parlors are covers for this pandemic."

The doctor glanced at Genesis. "Tell him."

"Tell me what?" Mr Lexmark's eyes roved over the two curiously.

"There are more of us." Dr Baden showed him the newspaper article they retrieved from the archive.

"They're on the way here as we speak. They too need to be protected until we can find a way to solve this mess. If not, their lives won't matter much either."

Mr Lexmark studied the grainy photograph taken by amateur video at the scene. He noticed the tattoo on the arm of one of the guys. "If what you're saying is true, this definitely proves a conspiracy theory."

"There's probably more all over the country. It's just we don't have access to the data," stated Dr Baden.

"When they get here you take them with you." He reached into his desk drawer and retrieved a cellphone. He handed the device to Dr Baden. "Take this. I'll be the only one to call on it." He turned off the tape recorder and stood. "I have a few things to do before the afternoon addition is finalized. Will you excuse me?"

Genesis and Dr Baden stood. They shook hands with Mr Lexmark and departed.

***

"Look! Right there! That's my friend Faith," exclaimed Genesis. She was genuinely excited. Genesis and Dr Baden sat in Mr Lexmark's vehicle. During the wait for the others to arrive, Genesis and the doctor discovered small intimate things about one another. It was easy for the two to share information ordinarily they wouldn't have. Genesis found him intriguing. He would be the oldest man she'd ever been with, and she anticipated the encounter. They sat for almost ninety minutes near the entrance of the building before Genesis spotted Faith and the group. Genesis rushed from the vehicle to intercept the group before they made it into the building. She did it without attracting unnecessary attention.

Faith spotted Genesis approaching. Her facial expression brightened. The two embraced compassionately for a moment. Faith introduced Genesis to the guys.

"I have a vehicle follow me." Genesis led the group to the vehicle. They were now mobile.

"I can't believe what's happening. Never would I believed we would be involved in something so scandalous. I knew something was wrong because killers we are not," stated Damian. Anger rose from within.

"Thankfully you were able to connect with us when you did. I think going to the newspaper is an excellent idea. It will give us the leverage we need to stay alive," said Dr Baden.

"How are you holding up Faith?" asked Genesis.

"Honestly, this is a lot to take in. Why would the government do this to its own citizens? What if no one ever discovered what's going on? The subjects would continue to believe they've committed awful crimes willingly. Never would they have known they were under control. The ones arrested would probably go on trial for violent acts. They would stand in front of a judge and be railroaded and given long prison sentences without any possible defense. Who's to say there aren't other victims out there?" Faith was obviously offended by what was happening.

Dr Baden remain silent as he concentrated on the roadway. His mind focused on a counter-attack.

41.

Detective Walters and Detective Byrd received calls from the homicide department. They headed toward a crime scene located in a motel. Normally, they wouldn't have been informed about such matters, but a blood sample identified as belonging to a suspect in a case under their jurisdiction is what linked them. They entered a room in disarray. Police activity was ongoing, a forensic task force worked to secure samples. Employees from the city's morgue were on standby waiting patiently for the opportunity to depart with two corpses. A uniformed officer approached the detectives.

"What do you have?" asked Detective Walters.

"We have two male bodies. One shot twice; the other once. We have blood and semen samples. Fingerprints tell us one of the victim's name is Oscar Hatchett. He has a record, mostly petty crimes. I guess fate caught up with him. We're doing ballistics on the shell casings left at the scene. I'm sure it will reveal more information."

The detectives neared a body, the cadaver was faced up. Detective Walters noticed blood underneath the body. "It appears he must have been turned over. Right here…" He pointed to a red smear on the sheet. "That must be lipstick. It probably happened when the body fell upon her. The weight must have smothered her on this spot. As you can see, the victim was shot in the back."

"Good observation." Detective Byrd stood over the other victim. He too was naked. "This guy has a surprise expression on his face. His eyes are wide open. That's pure anxiety mixed with adrenaline. He must have been going for something before he took two. The scratches on the table were made from fingernails." Detective Byrd reached into his jacket pocket and retrieved a pair of latex gloves. He placed them on and handled the digits of the deceased man. A knowingly smile ensued. Material under the corpse's fingernails were visible. Embedded between the nail and cuticle were wood splinters. The color matched perfectly with the table surface. "I'll bet he was reaching for a weapon."

"We know your suspect was here. What do you think made them come to New York?"

Detective Byrd's cellphone rang. "Hello?" He listened to the caller. "Okay, thank you." The line was disconnected. His attention was adverted to Detective Walters. "That was my people. They have information notifying the stepfather to one of the five boys in the basketball team slaying is also here in New York. We have navigation on his vehicle."

"I wonder what's going on? I'll get my people on it." He retrieved his cellphone and placed a call to headquarters. He could be heard giving out a series of orders.

***

Kenny Washington entered New York City via the George Washington Bridge. He drove through high volume traffic and parked his vehicle in a garage. He took to the streets on foot. Kenny was somewhat familiar with the city from his early days. He walked aimlessly down 7th Avenue toward downtown. The streets were saturated with yellow taxicabs, and the sidewalks were overcrowded with commuters. Everyone seemed to be in a hurry. Kenny approached a newspaper vendor and stopped. He picked up an early edition and read the headlines. The caption read CONSPIRACY! He read the article.

"Hey mister! This ain't a public library. Either you're purchasing or…"

Kenny eyed the clerk feeling self-conscious. "Sorry…" Kenny reached into his pocket and retrieved some bills. After purchasing the newspaper he continued onward. A mysterious inkling overwhelmed him. He sensed being watched. Kenny reflected on his younger years in the streets, and the same sensation always proved to be trustworthy keeping him safe. He glanced over his shoulder to see two men dressed in casual street attire staring at him. He looked away not wanting to draw attention. Kenny observed their shoes, the soft gum bottom tie-ups were a dead giveaway. *Cops! I wonder what they want with me? I'm not going to stand around to find out.* A yellow taxicab was passing. Kenny held out his hand and flag the vehicle. The taxicab stopped next to him. He quickly entered.

"Take me to the New York Times building."

42.

Zesty and Cheryl returned to the Port of Authority building. It was the place where their quest began. They headed directly for the storage lockers to retrieve, their personal belongings. Afterward, the duo approached a ticket counter. Cheryl purchased two one-way tickets to San Diego, California. The boarding time was close, and they hurried toward the departing ramp. Zesty was the first to spot them; she stopped dead in her stride. The sudden discontinuance of momentum resulted with her and Cheryl colliding.

"What's wrong?" asked Cheryl.

Zesty turned to face Cheryl. "Don't look, but two guys over there at one o'clock are cops. I'm sure of it."

Cheryl allowed her eyes to roam the area. She saw two men; both dressed in blue jeans, sneakers, and tee shirts. Both men wore leather jackets with bulges at the armpits. One had blonde hair; the other black. Both men were Caucasians.

Cheryl spoke in a soft tone. "I think they've noticed us because one of them is on his cellphone. The other is looking this way."

"Okay." Zesty sighed. "Don't make any sudden moves. There's an exit toward the left; near the restrooms. When I say go, make a dash for it. Are you ready?"

"Yes."

"Go!" In a quick decisive motion, Cheryl and Zesty dashed toward the exit. Zesty glanced over her shoulder to see the men were in pursuit. Adrenaline raced through the women's bloodstream as they entered the stairwell. The sound of patter on the metal stairs were pronounced. Cheryl was in the lead. Rushing down two flights of stairs, she forcefully opened an exit door. Zesty was close behind. They were now on a side street. The two glanced back. They were happy to see the pursuers were not in view. Zesty held up her hand to flag a taxicab. They entered the vehicle from the curbside.

"Driver take us to Brooklyn, just over the bridge," requested Zesty.

The vehicle picked up momentum. The two fearful women gazed out the windows watching for anything out of the norm. Zesty tried to regain her breathing as sweat cascaded down her forehead. Her heart felt as if it would jump out of her body. She peered over at Cheryl who seemed more in control emotionally. Cheryl's eyes were transfixed on an object ahead as they headed down 8th Avenue. A stream of green traffic lights were in their favor. It was at that moment the ladies began to relax. Cheryl erupted with an uncontrollable laughter. The tone of her laughter stemmed more from nervousness than merriment.

"What's so funny?" asked Zesty.

Cheryl tried to regain her composure. "You!" Laughter resumed. "I-I'm sorry, it's just the way you controlled the situation. I've never witnessed you in that light before. I'm usually the one having to have the answers. Tonight, besides the funny facial expressions you displayed, you were amazing." Her words were heartfelt. "I love you sister."

The vehicle made a sudden stop. Startled, the ladies gazed out of the window. An unmarked sedan converged on the taxicab as it crossed into the Chelsea district of the city. The same two men they spotted in the terminal were standing in front of the vehicle with weapons drawn. Identification badges were displayed in their free hands. They were shouting commands, but the sound was barely audible through closed windows. Simultaneously, each officer opened a rear passenger door. Outside noise flooded into the interior of the vehicle. Brisk air followed. Zesty shivered. She couldn't determine if the sudden tremble was from fear or coolness. The shouts of commands dominated the moment. Cheryl and Zesty became disoriented, the scene chaotic.

"Keep your hands where I can see them!" shouted the officer on Zesty's side.

"Slowly exit the vehicle! Walk toward the trunk and lean on it!" The blonde haired officer continued pointing his weapon. The driver of the taxicab was completely bewildered. He had no knowledge of what was transpiring. Fear, nervousness, and confusion controlled his emotions.

"What are you doing? We haven't done anything wrong!" exclaimed

Cheryl. She leaned over the trunk of the taxicab as instructed.

"Why did you run?" asked the blonde haired officer.

"I didn't know running was against the law."

"Very funny. You have the right to remain silent. Anything you say can and will be used against you in a court of law. You have a right to have a lawyer present. If you cannot afford one, a lawyer will be appointed to you free of charge. Do you understand what I have just said?" He nudged both women.

"Yeah," said Zesty.

"Yes, you still haven't told us why we are being held against our will," retorted Cheryl.

"For starters there's an all-point-bulletin out for your arrest."

Zesty and Cheryl were handcuffed and placed in the rear of an unmarked sedan.

43.

Park Slope is a well-kept residential area in Brooklyn. Spacious homes with manicured lawns were abundant. Tree lined streets were clean and quiet. A sports utility vehicle rolled into a garage. Everyone exited the vehicle and headed toward a Gothic-styled home. Entering through a sally port, a well-equipped kitchen with state-of-the-art appliances came in view. The decor was stainless steel and wood. They stepped into the living room; it too was elegantly decorated. Everyone gathered around.

"What's next?" asked Damian.

The group was quiet as they contemplated an answer. Dr Baden stepped forward.

"All we can do now is wait. When the media begin coverage, it will create a frenzy and stir things up. I've been assessing the situation. If they're able to control your physical bodies through the nerve system, what would stop them from doing it again?"

"You mean like make us turn against one another?" asked Genesis. She was completely skeptical.

"I'm not sure. What I do know is everyone needs a transfusion."

"Where can we get it done without drawing attention?"

Dr Baden paced as he contemplated the situation. "That's what I am figuring now. I need a place that can accompany all of you simultaneously."

Darkness triumphed over the day as evening approached. Dr Baden waited until dawn before executing his plan. He approached the rear of a huge brick building and tapped rhythmically on a glass door. The door was opened by a night janitor. The man was tall and slim in his early sixties, he wore basic eyeglasses atop his nose. The janitor's dark hue glistened off the crescent moon glow creating a dark-bluish tone to his already brown complexion. He wore a traditional janitorial uniform.

"Thank you Sam, I owe you."

Sam shook his head. "Dr Baden you don't owe anything. I've known you for twelve years. I don't know what is going on, and I don't really much want to. I'll be finished work in a few minutes, when you finish whatever your business is, just lock up." He gave the doctor an assuring wink and walked away. Dr Baden smiled as he returned to the vehicle. The others waited eagerly to hear the verdict. The entire entourage entered the quiet building. Footsteps resonated on the waxed tile floor.

"What is this place?" asked Genesis. She was curious because they entered through a rear exit.

"This is a blood bank." Dr Baden turned and looked toward the group. "I don't have much time to explain, please follow me." Dr Baden led them down a long corridor. Doors lined both sides of the hallway. They entered a set of stainless-steel doors. The interior resembled a sterile environment associated with a hospital. Padded tables were stationed in rows, curtains hung from tracks overhead to separate each station and to give privacy.

"I want everyone except Faith to find a table and be seated." Faith found her place next to the doctor as the others scrambled for a station. The doctor's attention was on Faith. "Faith, I'm going to need your assistance. It's quite simple. Watch me with the first one and repeat the same procedure with the others."

Faith stared at the machinery feeling intimidated. "I-I don't know if I can do it."

Dr Baden touched her shoulder reassuringly. "You'll do just fine." He walked toward Genesis' station and began removing items from a sterile container. Dr Baden placed a plastic tube in each of her arms. The tube end was equipped with a needle tip for injection into the vein. Another transparent tube was connected to a stainless-steel machine. The machine resembled a tiny dryer at a laundromat. Tubes aided to remove contaminated blood from the body. The doctor turned toward Faith. "All you do is place the tube in their arms and I'll set the dials." He watched as she took off to do his beck and calling. Dr Baden noticed her first stop was Damian. Understandably, he smiled. Dr Baden continued with the task at hand, and activated the machines. Each person sat reclined and engulfed in unified thoughts. *What's to become of me? Why me?*

After completing the task, Faith remained at Damian's side. He quietly watched his blood travel through a transparent tube into a machine. His filtered blood traveled painlessly though another tube for reentry into the body.

"What are you thinking about?" asked Faith. She was attracted to him.

Damian smiled and gazed into her eyes. Faith's face brightened his world. "Just the way fate has a way of throwing a curve; it also teaches something in the process."

"I want you to know I recognize the sacrifice you've made for me. I am very grateful. I was…" She succumbed to her emotions.

"Was what?" Damian smiled. He was intrigued with her shyness. Witnessing it for the first time amused him.

"Well…" She blushed. It was the most beautiful expression Damian had ever noticed on an individual. "I was wondering what were you gonna do when this is over?"

"Honestly? Things have been moving so fast I haven't had time to think about anything. I don't know what to think. I do know I'm glad we met."

It was Faith's turn to smile. "Let's get you better, then we can figure things out." Her smile brightened his mood.

Genesis stared into Dr Baden's eyes. "Do you think it'll work?"

He nodded confidently. "Yes, in fact it's working as we speak. You see those dials rotating? When they've completed a full revolution the process will be completed. I will have to keep samples from each of you in case it will be needed in the future. Right now the data show we are at seventy five percent toward purification."

"What then?"

The question caught him off guard. "What do you mean?" He didn't want to misconstrue what was meant by the question and he didn't want to sound insensitive.

"I mean where do we go from here?"

"Let's not worry about that now. Right now, let's concentrated on getting this stuff out of you. Afterwards, we'll have our entire lives to plan."

44.

Lieutenant Satchel entered a programming room where technicians adorned white laboratory attire. A huge monitor displayed a map of the United States. Dr Benjamin sat at a main terminal collecting data. He stopped working when he spotted the lieutenant and stood with an outstretched hand.

"Sir, I am glad you were able to make it. What can I do to help? It sounded urgent on the telephone."

After the greeting subsided, the two sat at the control terminal adjacent to one another. Lieutenant Satchel gestured for the technician to come closer.

"The information I have is classified. I couldn't mention it over on the telephone." The lieutenant's voice was a whisper. "What if I asked you to abort? To pull the plug on the subjects in the quadrants of the United States?"

Dr Benjamin's eyebrows moved as he listened to the request. "Why would you want to do that? Things are working fine. I thought this project was an ongoing process to receive pertinent data."

"I understand, but can you do it?"

"I'm not sure how the process would be received by the hosts. It may terminate their lives."

"Doesn't matter, do it!"

***

Detective Byrd entered the interrogation room while Detective Walters remained outside gazing in through a two-way mirror. Zesty and Cheryl sat adjacent to one another looking exhausted and scared.

"Why did you run? I've checked your records and they're clean."

"I knew no one would believe me."

"Shut up Zesty!" interjected Cheryl. She was trying to keep her from incriminating herself.

Zesty glanced at her friend; she was not prepared to let Cheryl take a fall on her behalf. "No!" Her attention was adverted to the detective. "I don't believe any of it either. For the record, I did it alone. Cheryl here is just my friend tagging along. She has no part in it."

"So you admit to killing Stax?"

"Yes, I just don't remember doing it. I know it sounds crazy. I think I was being controlled."

Detective Byrd glanced toward the two-way mirror. He knew Detective Walters was listening in on what was being said. "How about the hotel?"

Cheryl was about to answer. Zesty interrupted. "That also," she stated convincingly.

"Then why is it we found only her DNA at the crime scene? We found some on the bed mixed with blood and fecal matter. Also on a champagne bottle neck?"

"As I told you, I can't remember. I called her to pick me up."

"So that your story?" Detective Byrd stared at the two.

"Yes."

He shrugged his shoulders. "Okay, suit yourself." He stood and exited the room. The ladies were left alone. Detective Byrd entered the outer room to speak with Detective Walters.

"Let me have a word with them." He headed into the interrogation room and closed the door behind. He had the opportunity to observe their demeanors. Detective Walters took a seat facing the women and noticed disconcertment.

"What do you want? To nail the coffin shut?" asked Cheryl.

"No, I heard what you said and I believe you." He watched her eyes widen with suspicion. "Let me tell you what I know. First, can I see your recent tattoos?

The ladies looked to one another questionably. "I know what you're thinking. Good-cop bad-cop." He stood to examine the artwork. "This is what I know…" Detective Walters began explaining the information he discovered concerning the coincidental outbreaks of violence around the country at the time of her incident.

Zesty was devastated after hearing the information. It was the first explanation that made any sense to her since the occurrence. "So what do we do now? If you believe we're innocent what's next?"

"We need more proof. Don't worry, I'm going to find it."

45.

Four high ranking officers sat in a conference room located in a secured building in Washington, DC. Each person represented a different branch of the armed forces. A meeting of the minds was underway. The subject, Lieutenant Satchel, was not in attendance. His absence was an intentional deploy by the group. The impromptu meeting was called recently.

General Major Weatherby represented the Army, he tossed a copy of the New York Times newspaper onto the table. "How could this have happened?"

General Carson represented the Marines. He picked up the publication, silently read the caption story, and passed it to the next person. "It doesn't state any names as of yet."

"It implicates the defense department," stated the Air Force representative.

"Okay, don't get panicky. We have safeguards in place. That's why we have Lieutenant Satchel. The project is in his command, he's our fall guy."

"I say we terminate any data that link Project i-Ink to us. We'll all be finished if this gets out. I'm not ready to risk everything I've worked for on this. Are you?" The group shook their heads in agreement.

"I say we send someone to pay that New York Times editor a little visit," requested General Major Weatherby. "We can't afford any prowling into this."

"It may be too late. If we're reading this, you best believe others are also."

"He's right, we may have to act fast before there's an inquiry into the matter."

***

Telephones constantly rang in the editor's office, the switchboard console was lit with awaiting calls. A frenzy started after the story was released. Chief Editor Dennis Lexmark spoke to the executives from major governmental departments about national security. A knock came to the door.

"Enter."

A beautiful woman with natural auburn hair and a shapely figure entered. "Mr Lexmark, I'm sorry to bother. There's a persistent gentleman here to see you. His name is Kenny Washington. He says his son is one of the five basketball players in your article," announced the secretary.

Mr Lexmark held the receiver to his ear. "I'll call you back, something just came up." He replaced the receiver on the cradle. Mr Lexmark adverted his attention to his secretary. "Please, send him in." Mr Lexmark stood in anticipation of Mr Washington's arrival with an outstretched hand. "Have a seat. Can I get you something to drink?" Kenny declined the offer. "How can I help you?"

"The article in your paper, that's my boy you're talking about. Please, can you tell me where I may find him? His mother is worried to death of his whereabouts. What is this all about?"

"As far as I know…" Mr Lexmark explained what he learned. He informed Kenny his son was safe and wrote the address on a piece of paper. "Remember, you must make sure you're not followed."

***

Later that evening, Mr Lexmark turned off the lights in his office in preparation to leave. His department had long been gone, and the night janitors were the only signs of life on the floor as they cleaned offices. Mr Lexmark exited the office and locked the door. Without warning, he felt a hand grip him from behind. The grasp was strong and he was no match for the attacker. A cloth was placed over his nose and mouth; a sweet pungent odor permeated his nostrils before he lost consciousness.

Through a huge drain pipe erected deep in the earth, bright light illuminated. Cold wind hovered overhead along with echo sounds of birds. Suddenly startled, the birds deviated from a flight path and headed down the hollow tube. The sensation of being pricked was overwhelming; hard violent beaks pecked his face.

SMACK!

The impact of the slap across Dennis Lexmark's face returned him to the moment. He took in the sight of a dim lit enclosure. Dampness and chilled temperatures filled the unfamiliar area.

"Now you listen. Who gave you the information used in your article? Don't lie!"

Dennis Lexmark looked at the antagonist who wore dark clothing. The stranger's face was hidden by a mask; his hands were also covered. Dennis was barred from visualizing the ethnicity of his oppressor. Fear showered over the chief editor in the form of perspiration. He realized he was restrained to a chair. "I wasn't the one that printed the story."

"You're the chief editor, that means you oversee all articles before they get to press. It's your job to make sure the stories are written in a way to keep the company from being liable. I'll ask you one more time before the torture begins. Where did you get the link between your story and the tattoo parlor?"

It wasn't what was asked that scared Mr Lexmark the most, it was the calm and steady tone of the stranger's voice. "I told you, I'm chief editor…"

"Okay, that's your story?" The mysterious man removed a single-edged razor blade from his pocket. Dennis looked on terrified. *What have I gotten myself into?*

The masked man removed a clear bottle of transparent liquid from a case and unsheathed the razor. He unscrewed the top from the bottle releasing a pungent odor. The scent was immediately identified by Mr Lexmark's nostrils. *Isopropyl alcohol, rubbing alcohol.* His mind computed the intent. Matching the highly volatile liquid with a well-honed blade meant only one thing to Dennis Lexmark. He trembled in his seat anticipating forthcoming pain. The chief editor struggled to free himself but to no avail. The masked man neared with both items. Dennis' eyes scanned the room looking for an escape, and noticed the location was cold and filled with debris. *It's probably an abandoned facility.* His ears didn't detect any outside sounds. "Help! Help!" The energy used to yelled at the top of his lungs depleted him.

"No use in screaming, no one can hear you from here. Let me tell you something. You must have pissed someone off real bad for them to involve me. For me this is all business. If I were you, I'd make it easy on myself." He took the well-honed blade and made a small incision in the editor's right forearm. The cut was a quarter inch in length. The torturer poured a capful of the clear liquid onto the cut.

"Aaahh!" Agony intensified. The pain subsided as the liquid quickly evaporated. His breathing was sporadic. "I told…"

Another incision was made on the other forearm. The torturer poured alcohol slowly into a small cap, allowing Dennis to anticipate the forthcoming torment.

"Okay, okay. I'll tell you…" He began telling the story to the masked man. "They're at my house." He gave the man the information to his address.

"Wasn't that simple? You could have saved yourself a lot of pain."

Mr Lexmark looked on perplexed. "W-what now? I told you what you wanted. Please, let me go. I promise not to tell anyone. I haven't seen your face, there's nothing I can say even if I wanted to."

Holding a scalpel, the torturer stared at Mr Lexmark. He approached and removed his mask. Mr Lexmark's eyes became fearful as he stared at a young kid half his age. His features included a clean shaven face, sandy brown hair, and greenish-blue eyes. He appeared less menacing to Dennis. *Maybe I'll make it out of here.* Another thought occurred. *If he is showing me his face, it could mean only one thing…* The notion brought an unholy dread. Lexmark's body was drenched in sweat at the sight of the scalpel.

The tormentor smiled exposing yellowed teeth. "You've guest it!" In a single fluid motion, the tormentor pulled on Mr Lexmark's bottom lip, and passed the surgically sharp blade slightly over the surface of Lexmark's inner lip. The scalpel cut with precision separating tissue, but not sever. As blood gushed, duct tape was placed over Lexmark's mouth. The intruder gathered his belongings and exited.

Things happened fast for Dennis; he was confused to the entire situation. A sweet acrid taste filled his mouth, it was the taste of his own blood. Pain grew intensely. He now understood why the stranger placed duct tape over his mouth. Mr Lexmark began gagging on his own fluid. Choking sensation overwhelmed him as blood gushed forcefully into his mouth. His reflex muscle couldn't swallow the liquid fast enough, causing the blood to searched for an exit. Fluid rushed through his nostrils forcefully, blocking Lexmark's air flow.

Dennis Lexmark's death was atrociously painful. He was left in an unknown location with his eyes gaped opened; his face and clothing saturated with blood.

***

A commercial roofing truck came to a full stop in front of a specific address in the Park Slope section of Brooklyn. Three men wearing blue denim coveralls exited the van. Each man carried a tool case along with a duffle bag on their shoulders. Their identities were obscured with the use of dark eyewear and caps. A lock pick was used to gain access inside the house. The group passed through a foyer to a huge living room. The men unfastened the duffle bags and removed automatic weapons from within. Metallic clatter from magazines being engaged resonated. The men used sign language to communicate, each person searched a different location for occupants.

The death squad met in the living room, the search of the house was fruitless. The men exited the house in an organized manner and reloaded the vans with their equipment before driving away down the quiet residential block.

46.

Kenny Washington drove to the address the chief editor gave him and parked midway on the block before turning off the engine. Kenny sat in the rear compartment eyeing the activity on the quiet street. The residential area was clear of pedestrian traffic, but noticed an out of place vehicle ahead. A commercial truck was parked in front of the home. *Hmm...* Hairs on the nape of his neck tingled; a strong distrusting inkling existed. The license plate was government issued. Kenny remained inside the vehicle and watched a group of men exited the house dressed in coveralls; each carried a tool box and duffle bag. Kenny sensed something odd about the situation. He noticed their boots were military issue, and their identities were obscure with the use of dark eyewear and caps. He watched as they enter the vehicle and drove away. Silhouettes of their features were all he could see. Afraid to move, Kenny remained in his vehicle. He waited until the truck was long gone before he continued onto the block. He drove to the address and knocked on the door. No one answered. He knocked again. The sound of feet shuffling behind the door was audible. The door opened.

Faith studied the stranger in front of her. She looked up and down the quiet block for anything out of the ordinary. She wasn't worried because the guys were standing behind the door.

"Hello?" Faith opened the door partially.

Kenny was taken aback at the attractive young woman. "Hi, my name is Kenny Washington. I was referred here by Mr Dennis Lexmark. I have a son named Damian who I'm told is here."

Faith continued to eye the stranger, she scrutinized the scene by studying his body language. Mr Lexmark's name being mentioned caused her to slightly relax. Faith continued to stare at Kenny. After hearing Damian's name mentioned, she sensed the authenticity in his words. *For him to know those names it must be true.* She stepped aside allowing Kenny access into the house.

Kenny entered and saw the group next to her. They entered through a foyer. Kenny studied the high vaulted ceilings and the extravagant decor of the house as he stepped into the living room. He was met by a group of people, some were strangers.

Damian was startled at the sight of Kenny, he never thought he'd be happy to see a familiar face as he was now. He approached Kenny feeling mixed emotions, their last encounter displayed aggression. Damian was now delighted to see him. The two embraced. The others looked on quietly. Not knowing why, Faith felt empathy for the two, she felt an indescribable bond was at work. Kenny was happy to be reunited with Damian. For the first time, he felt relief from the ill-feelings he harbored between his wife and Damian. Compassion melted away all mixed emotions as he realized he was wanted and needed. The embrace lasted longer than expected. Kenny thought strongly to call Clair and enlighten her with the latest news. Damian gazed into his eyes. "How did you find us?"

Kenny looked around at the others and explained his plight, he started with the navigation system. He expounded on how he was led to New York. "That's how it happened. Now tell me what is this all about, and how are you involved in this mess? Do you have any idea what the newspapers are saying? You guys are being referred to as murderers. Not to mention what this is doing to all of your parents."

"Dad..." Damian couldn't believe he used the phrase. "Let me introduce you to Faith, Dr Baden, and Genesis. You know the gang here." His crew and the others greeted. The introduction was cordially accepted by everyone.

"Mr Washington, I want to mention that Damian is playing himself down. He saved my life," asserted Faith.

"I think we should make plans to leave this place. I don't think it's safe."

Dr Baden became inquisitive. "What makes you say that?" Everyone's attention was now on Kenny as they anticipated a response.

"As I arrived, I witnessed three men returning from here. They were disguised as roofers, only they were out of sync with their boots. They were military-styled. I noticed the license plate was government issued. They looked like professionals."

Everyone looked to one another bewildered. "How could they have known?" asked Dr Baden. A notion entered his mind. *Take this…I'll be the only one to call.* He recalled the prior conversation with Mr Lexmark. Dr Baden retrieved the cellphone given to him by Mr Lexmark and dialed. There was no answer, he called the office. The doctor listened to secretary explain a situation. Dr Baden's facial expression changed. Overwhelmed with emotions, the cellphone dropped from his hand. Dr Baden collapsed as tears fell from his eyes. His legs trembled as he cowered his face with his hands. Stan moved swiftly to support the doctor and escorted him to a couch.

Genesis rushed to his aid. "What's wrong baby?" Everyone heard the endearment in her words and eyed one another momentarily.

Dr Baden's eyes were laden with tears. "He's dead."

"Who's dead?"

"Dennis Lexmark. His secretary said they found his body in an abandoned building. He was tortured." Grief consumed him.

The group was in awe, they couldn't believe what was said.

"What are we gonna do now?" asked Dexter. Fear entered his being.

"I say we get out of here. If they've gotten to him, there's no telling what information was given. They might return looking for us. We can't afford to take that chance," stated Damian. He faced the group. "Everyone get your belongings, we'll take both vehicles." The group stood unsure. "Now! Let's go!"

47.

Zesty and Cheryl remained in the county jail while Detective Walters and Detective Byrd investigated more of the story. They were placed in a five by eight foot cell with steel bars. The enclosure was designed for double occupancy. Steel bunk beds, a stainless-steel toilet-sink combo, and a polished metal mirror was all that filled the space. The ladies were made to change into bright yellow jumpsuits with the jail's monogram stenciled on the back in black letters. The sound of prison activity was animate; inmates yelled through bars communicating with prisoners located in separate areas of the cell block. The acoustics in the corridor echoed the sound. Steel doors slammed in the cell block along with static eruptions from two-way radios carried by the officers.

"What do you think will happen to us?" asked Zesty. She paced the small confined space. Cheryl was on the bottom bunk staring up at the underside of the top bunk reading scratched words underneath, scribble left behind by other prisoners. Cheryl thought of it as mindless doodle and idiotic slogans from other unfortunate souls.

"I don't know. All you had to do was keep your mouth shut!"

"Then what? I couldn't sit back and allow you to take the heat."

"What good did that do any of us? We're both here."

"I'm sorry Cheryl."

Cheryl sat up and stared at her friend. "At least we're still together, that's all that matters. Why don't you rest? You're going to need your strength for tomorrow."

Zesty stopped pacing after contemplating what was said. She climbed the rungs of the ladder attached to the metal bunk. Reaching the top, she flopped on a thin plastic mattress. Cheryl heard a deep sigh emit from her friend. "I promise you, no matter the outcome we'll endure it together."

***

Lieutenant Satchel watched as technician Benjamin commanded the staff in the control center to certain duties. The technician gazed at the lieutenant.

"Sir, we're all set and waiting your final command. I must advise you it must be done in sequence. Because of the irregularity of the request, we don't have enough data to know the after effects."

"Just do it!" exclaimed the lieutenant.

The technician studied the monitor, a map of the United States was graphically displayed. Hundreds of yellow and green dots were distributed across the country. He concentrated his efforts on the eastern section of the country. A series of adjustments were made, data from the computer gave him constant up-to-date logistics. A master switch was pressed. Central United States was the main focus, next was the southern part. The technician pushed his seat away from the console and stood.

"I hope the right thing is being done sir."

Lieutenant Satchel nodded in approval. "Yes, it's the right thing to do." Both men now waited for results.

48.

Pandemonium erupted across the United States; sheer panic and violence were widespread. News medias talked of an undetectable terrorist attacks. Epic proportions of the country were hit simultaneously. Vicious assaults resulted with massive bodies left in its wake. Never has there been a report of this magnitude on American soil. After the 911 World Trade Center attack, the government done everything in its power to assure safety to the American people. Now this. No organization came forward to claim responsibility for the damages. The Center for Disease Control, (CDC), was called in to ascertain the situation. It was thought to be another strain of the Covid-19 virus. Police, emergency workers, firemen, and national guardsmen were called to help regain control from looters and violent mayhem occurring throughout the country. The President of the United States was notified. He in turn notified the Department of Defense. A telephone conference with four high-ranking military officials came to a conclusion.

"The project is no longer containable. It's time to implement Project Bail Out." Everyone agreed.

***

Exiting a military aircraft, Lieutenant Satchel was met by four military police officers. They saluted him. He explained the nature of the visit and was caught off guard with the outcome. He was restrained and led to an awaiting unmarked vehicle and whisked away.

***

Detective Byrd didn't know what to make of the situation. Detective Walters believed a link existed with all the madness and decided to visited a few crime scenes. Detective Walters came to a conclusion, he observed in many of the events the aggressors didn't realize their actions. From experience as a detective, he sensed their statements were genuine. Detective Byrd was frustrated not knowing exactly what was taking place, he was fully convinced they were experiencing a foreign terror attack. What unsettled him most was not being able to figure Zesty and Cheryl's role into the mix of things.

Detective Walters was astounded at the discoveries; each body depicted identical tattoo markings. He couldn't retain the excitement of his findings. He stooped near the body of a victim in an ally. Rigor mortis had set in; swelling from internal gases inflated the corpse. He looked around noticing an abundance of graffiti on public property. Trash strewn on the seedy residential street was an eyesore. The detective noticed the deceased died with open eyes. "Detective Byrd can you come over for a moment?"

Detective Byrd was communicating with an officer. He excused himself and found his way to where Detective Walters was standing. "What do you have?"

"Tell me what you see."

Detective Byrd studied the body. He turned to his partner to get a clue. There was none. Feeling dumbfounded, he shrugged his shoulders. "I don't get it."

"The tattoo is the same as the others, there must be some truth to this theory. Dr Baden may have been onto something. I say we visit a few of those tattoo parlors with search warrants."

Detective Byrd smiled as he remembered Zesty and Cheryl wearing identical tattoos. The news enlightened him, he didn't want to arrest the ladies because his intuition told him they were innocent. They were only trying to earn a legitimate living. "I'm with you. Let's check out the parlors." He gestured by flashing his badge. "We'll worry about the warrants later." A sly winked followed. His cellphone rang. "Detective Byrd homicide…" He listened attentively without interruption. "Okay, I'll be there shortly." The line was disconnected. His attention was aim toward Detective Walters. "They have my two perps in custody.

"Since they're not going anywhere, do you want to continue to the parlor first?"

"Yeah, maybe we'll gather more information that will make dealing with them easier."

49.

Sunrise ascended over the horizon as morning dew blanketed the town. A two-vehicle convoy travelled on a main street heading toward the interstate. The lead vehicle was driven by Dr Baden. Genesis, Faith, and Damian were passengers. Kenny Washington trailed close behind in his vehicle. Dexter sat next to him with Stan, Chuck, and Rufus in the rear. The group was quiet. Everyone seemed focused on their own thoughts. Kenny's vision was on the desolate roadway. He turned on the radio; the sound of an announcer's voice cut through the tense ambiance with a breaking news report. The subject was on the violent outbreaks across the country. The CDC was called to investigate the situation.

"I wonder what's really going on?" asked Kenny. The question was not directed to anyone in particular.

"Maybe this is bigger than what the doctor thought," responded

Stan.

"Where are we going?" asked Dexter. He nervously nibbled on his fingernails and cuticles.

"They're probably using GPS to track everyone," stated Chuck.

The statement triggered an alarm in Kenny's mind. "That's it!" Everyone was startled by the outburst. "I have tracking on my vehicle!" Kenny honked his horn in effort to gain Dr Baden's attention.

"What's going on?" asked Dexter.

Kenny adverted his attention from the road to Dexter. "We have to abandon these vehicles. They can pinpoint our location through satellite. That's how I found you guys."

Genesis rode up front with Dr Baden. Faith and Damian were in the rear. Faith rested her head on his shoulder. Everyone's attention was adverted to the noise of a honking horn. Dr Baden gazed into his rear view mirror to see Kenny flashing his headlights to gain attention. Everyone aboard became inquisitive.

"I wonder what he want?" asked Dr Baden. He used his turn signal and steered the vehicle toward the road shoulder. Kenny followed suit.

Both vehicles came to a complete stop. The drivers converged with one another between the two idling vehicles. A strong scent of exhaust fumes was pronounced.

"What is it?" asked Dr Baden. "Is everyone all right?"

"Yes, it's nothing like that. We have to abandon my vehicle quickly. They can pinpoint our location through the navigation system. That's

Jackie McConnell

how I located the vehicle when I thought it was stolen."

"I understand. Let's get everyone into my vehicle."

"What if they're looking for Mr Lexmark's vehicle. I'm sure they've covered all bases."

"What do you propose we do?"

"Because of the seriousness of the matter they will have all of the main roads, trains, and airports covered. I think the best place to hide is in plain sight, at least until the smoke clears."

Dr Baden smiled. "I think you're right. We'll take these vehicles off road and find another means of transportation." The two returned to the vehicles to inform the others of the latest plan.

The convoy continued toward the nearest town. They parked the vehicles at an undisclosed location near a state park. The scenery was picturesque; beautiful greenery and trees were perfect cover for the group. Beyond spruce trees, the group spotted a business area across from a strip mall. What captured everyone's interest was a car rental station. There were dozens of vehicles on a lot.

Dr Baden turned toward Faith. "This isn't your fight. You don't have to continue on, but if you decide to we could use your help."

Faith looked into Damian's eyes and turned toward the others. "No! That's where you're wrong, this is my fight. What do you want me to do?"

Everyone observed the display of remarkable courage. Dr Baden continued. "If what we know is accurate, they'll be looking for only us. You are not on the radar. You can be our face, ears, and eyes. You see that rental station behind those trees? I need for you to go inside and purchase a vehicle that will be able to accommodate all of us.

One that will not draw attention."

"We'll need cash. We are pretty low," stated Damian.

Everyone began searching their pockets for cash. Damian gathered the money and handed it to Faith.

"That's not necessary, I have my credit card."

"No, we don't want to leave a paper trail. Cash is better," stated Damian. Faith understood.

"Okay, I'll do it."

A black conversion van with cut-out windows stopped near the side entrance of the park. For a moment everyone was edgy to the strange vehicle approaching. Faith exited the vehicle, the sight of her eased everyone's anxiety. Having a female driving was more appealable.

"Where are we headed?"

"Get on the interstate and head south."

50.

Detective Walters and Detective Byrd entered a tattoo parlor called Urban Ink World. They were amazed at the crowd assembled inside the establishment. Patrons waited in line to be tattooed. Detective Byrd blended with the patrons viewing glass displays filled with designs. Detective Walters approached a reception are where a man wearing blue jeans and a company shirt stood and greeted.

"May I help you?"

He produced his identification. "I'm Detective Walters, is there a place we can talk in private?"

The clerk nervously browsed the room. "How about my customers?"

"You needn't worry about that. My partner will watch out for things. It'll only take a moment of you time."

"What is this about?"

"Shall we?" The detective gestured toward the rear of the shop.

The backroom was used as a storage area. A windowless room held a small desk, two chairs, and desktop computer. A few file cabinets were in a corner. The men faced.

"I need to use your computer terminal. I'm here officially, a murder suspect wearing tattoos we believe were created here. Please log on and allow me to see the recent completed customer data. It will only take a moment. In fact, you can go deal with your customers and I won't be long."

"Okay." The clerk logged in. Afterward, he exited the room leaving the detective alone to his own demise.

Detective Walters went to work on the terminal using the information he obtained from Dr Baden. As he viewed the data on the monitor, Detective Walters carefully read. He exited the room into a frenzy of patrons awaiting service. Detective Byrd nodded toward Detective Walters, and the two headed outside.

Clamorous street noise were at high decibel levels. Pungent odor of soot and exhaust fumes lingered in the air.

"What did you find out?" asked Detective Byrd.

"Exactly what we thought." He retrieved a document from his jacket and handed it to his partner.

Detective Byrd read the information. "We now have a name. This thing is getting interesting, maybe this is above our pay-grade. Are you sure you want to continue down this rabbit hole?"

"Yes, those girls are innocent and we need the proof to prove it."

Detective Byrd sighed. "Okay, suit yourself. Where to now?"

"It says here Lieutenant Satchel is out of Washington, DC."

"District of Columbia it is…"

***

The detention center was quiet in the late night hour. Restful snores echoed through the dim corridor. Occasional sounds of footsteps from guards doing tours were the only activity in the building. Cheryl and Zesty found sleep easy, exhaustion overwhelmed them from the long and drawn out day. Without warning, a sound of impaired breathing erupted in the cell. Both women displayed rapid eye movements as a bitter taste filled their mouths and caused their body temperatures to elevate drastically. Zesty's vivid daydream took on another dimension. While asleep on the top bunk, she experienced Stax's hands around her throat. Her life slowly ebbed away as his vise grip hands squeezed. She fought with all of her might, but his hands were too powerful for her to resist. Zesty's mind conjured an idea for escape. She relinquished her grip as his hands tightened around her neck. Her thumbs dug deep into the corners of his eye sockets. Zesty felt soft tissue collapse under pressure, a dull pop resonated as her fingers became saturated with blood. Stax screamed in dreadful anguish. Using her last ounce of strength, she shoved him away. Stax gripped her hand as he fell toward an abyss. In the conscious world, Zesty ejected herself from the top bunk onto the hard concrete floor. As she descended, her head hit a side rail. The impact twisted her neck at an unnatural angle, and her skull cracked upon contact with the concrete floor. A dull thud sound was associated with the fall, the noise resembled a watermelon falling to the ground from an elevated height. Her devastated demise was painless. The foreign substance in her system did exactly what it was designed to do, cause the host to self-destruct.

The atrocious death of Zesty went unnoticed by Cheryl who was under the same psychological attack from the neuro agent coursing through her system. The deadly substance thandiasine was activated with the use of ultra violet rays distributed from a satellite miles above the earth. Cheryl's dilemma was quite different. Her body consumed a high frequency from the satellite's boost. The force sent electrical currents through her body. The results? A shrill scream emitted from her that shattered the tranquil in the cellblock. Cheryl's eyes opened abruptly. Disoriented, she bolted from her bunk. Unaware of her fallen friend, Cheryl stood facing the dark cold bars. The sounds of footsteps upon the hard floor crescendoed; voices from staff rushing to investigate was prominent. Squelches from two-way radios, footsteps, and keys added to the disruption. A female officer was the first to reach Cheryl's cell. Her eyes widened as she witnessed the gruesome scene. She saw the bloodied body of a victim on the floor. Her cellmate was standing near screaming. A group of officers, male and female, converged on the scene. As the first officer unlocked the cell door and swung the gate open, Cheryl rushed toward the officer with gleam in her eyes. Her pupils were dilated, and her stare was straightforward. Cheryl was in a mesmeric trance. Her mind was divided and unaware of her true surroundings. She envisioned unimaginable creatures. Cheryl placed both hands around the throat of the officer. The others responded with force. Wooden clubs came across Cheryl's back. Being under neurologic control, she didn't experience the pain associated with such impact on the body. She continued strangling the creature. Cheryl saw fire emit from the nostril of the creature. In her mind, the creature favored a human dragon. Another officer responded with lethal force. He aimed his taser gun, the weapon was set at fifty thousand volts, and pulled the trigger. A wire attached barb sent electrical current into Cheryl's body; high voltage hit nerve centers. The most sensitive was the heart muscle, causing her heart to constrict without release. Cheryl suffered a massive heart attack. She release her grip and fell to the floor unmoving. She was dead before her body hit the concrete floor. Other officers on scene took no chances with her feigning an unconscious behavior and shackled her arms behind her back.

"What the hell was that about?" asked the rescued officer.

"She must have killed this one and decided to escape when you opened the cell door," stated another officer.

"Call the infirmary and the warden," commanded the rescued officer. She rubbed the soreness from her neck.

***

Detective Walters and Detective Byrd landed at Maryland-Baltimore-Washington Airport. A light mist blanketed the city. Both men were dressed in dark colored suits and topcoats to ward off the elements. The pair entered a taxicab. Detective Walters requested to be taken to the Department of Defense. They sat separated from the driver by a thick plexiglass partition.

"I think we're making headway. This proves what Zesty and Cheryl said actually has merit. After this meeting, I'm going to release those ladies. They're going to be living proof to these claims," said Detective Walters.

"I guess you're right, let's see what happens."

A ringtone reverberated in the confine space. Both men reached for their cellphones simultaneously. Detective Walters pressed the receiving button on his device.

"Yeah." He listened attentively without any interruptions. "Okay, I'll be there first thing in the morning." He disconnected the line. He gazed out of the window at the moving scenery.

"What is it?" Detective Byrd detected a change in the detective's demeanor.

"The two suspects are dead."

"Dead? How?" asked Detective Byrd. The news was unexpected.

"It seem as if one killed the other. The survivor was killed as she tried to attack a guard in effort to escape."

"That sounds strange. It doesn't fit their modus operandi." Detective Byrd was drained of emotions. *What the hell is going on?* His mind contemplated the scenario. "I just got back the test results. The information I received is the chief editor of the New York Times was found dead."

51.

The conversion van handled nicely on the roadway as they continued on the interstate heading south. A tollbooth loomed ahead. Faith guided the vehicle to a smooth stop at a wooden gate. She passed the clerk a bill and waited patiently for the change. The passage lantern changed from red to green just as the clerk handed her the correct currency. The vehicle continued onward. The passengers in the vehicle were quiet; some held their breaths in anticipation of trouble as they passed the toll booth. Everyone began to relax as they moved onward.

"Do you really think going to Washington, DC will solve our problems?" asked Chuck. He was skeptical of the entire ordeal.

Dr Baden answered. "With the blood samples as proof, we'll be able to make a case."

"How's that? You're also wanted by the authorities. Remember?"

The interior of the vehicle resumed silence once again. "I can do it," interjected Faith. She kept her eyes on the roadway as she spoke. "After all, you did say I would be your eyes, ears, and body. I might as well be your brains too."

Her request was being contemplated by the others. Damian realized he influenced her decision. A part of him couldn't allow her to involve herself. Faith wanted to do what she could for her friend Genesis and the others, she felt their union wasn't by chance. She realized the significance. *Beside, I like him.* Faith gazed into Damian's eyes.

"Okay, I'll brief you with a mock interview as you drive," stated Dr Baden.

Sharp chirps from a police cruiser erupted. Caution and alarm ceased the moment.

"What happened?" asked Dr Baden.

"What did you do?" asked Stan.

Faith became agitated. "I didn't do anything! They just appeared." She studied the activity through the side view mirror.

"Okay, everyone calm down. We'll play it smooth. Remember, we're students visiting Washington, DC." He turned toward Faith. "Just be easy and pull over to the shoulder. When he approaches show him your identification. We'll take it from there." Damian stated.

The vehicle was manned by a lone state trooper. The officer exited the cruiser and placed on a wide brim hat as he proceeded to approach the vehicle.

Faith watched his reflection through the mirror noticing he wore dark aviator sunglasses. Faith also noticed he kept a hand near his holstered weapon. "He's coming this way." She was obviously nervous.

"Just be cool and don't panic." Damian's voice was a whisper.

The officer tapped on the driver side window. Faith touched a button that allowed the the glass to descend. "Yes officer."

"Please turn off the engine and show me your license, registration, and insurance card."

The officer observed closely as Faith slowly reached in her pocket for her wallet. She produced one of the documents requested; her driver license.

"Where is the registration and insurance card?"

"This here is a rental. We are students on our way to Washington, DC. We're on an observational field trip."

The officer gazed at Damian. His stare returned to Faith. "Look inside of the glove compartment, that's usually where the company store the documents." The officer waited while she reached for the documents. He kept a keen eye on the two. Once the glove compartment was opened, the officer leaned to the side to peer inside. Faith received the two documents and handed them to the officer.

The officer studied the documents for a brief moment. "Excuse me, this will only take a moment." He returned to his vehicle with the documents in hand.

Faith looked around at the others. "Now what?"

"You're doing fine. Just remain calm." Genesis' voice was a whisper.

Faith watched the officer enter his vehicle from the rear view mirror. "He's probably calling in the plate number."

"It's okay. That's why you were the best candidate for the assignment," said Dr Baden.

The trooper returned and handed the documents to Faith. "I stopped you because your garment is trapped between the door."

Faith glanced out the window to see her jacket was wedged, she released the garment by opening the door. "Thank you."

"Drive safe." The officer returned to his cruiser.

Sighs of relief became audible from the group, everyone was glad the ordeal was over. Faith placed the vehicle in gear and continued onward. Kenny thought about Clair and decided to call.

***

Clair moved about the house a nervous wreck. She'd been emotionally trapped since Damian's disappearance. Staggering news reports about her son and his group of friends were disconcerting. The added report of violence around the country only confused and frightened her more as anxiety set deep within. Clair awakened with a throbbing headache; she stared at her image in the mirror noticing her eyes were red and puffy. Clair was unable to remember Kenny's cellphone number. She sat in the kitchen nursing a cup of black coffee when the phone rang. She picked it up the receiver hastily and knocked over the cup of coffee in the process. "Damn it!" she exclaimed. "Hello? Damian? Kenny?" She listened and realized she was holding her breath. Hearing the familiar voice allowed her the pleasure of breathing. "Where are you? Do you know I'm here worried to death? Did you find Damian?" Clair listened to the response as relief enveloped her. Kenny's voice dismissed unsure thoughts of being alone. The response felt as if a weighted object had been lifted from around her heart. She was now able to feel a glimpse of hope. "Please, put him on." Tears flowed down her cheeks as she listened to her precious son's voice. "When are you coming home?" She listened to the reply. "No! Come home now!" Clair couldn't contain her emotions any longer. She felt a sense of guilt after the outburst. "Please, get here soon." The line was disconnected. Clair resumed cleaning up the place for her family's safe return. Her first thought was to have a private surprise reception awaiting their return.

***

Kenny and Damian studied one another's facial expressions after talking with Clair. They actually felt an invisible bond. They realized they needed one another. Clair's happiness was top priority to both men.

"Why don't you go on home. We can tie things over in Washington," requested Damian to Kenny. The group quietly listened to the two-way conversation.

"I know why you're saying that. Thanks, but no thanks. I think I'll stay around until everyone get out of this mess. I'm sure your mom will be happier with all three of us coming home together."

Damian was unsure of Kenny's meaning. "You mean the two of us. Right?"

Kenny's smile was wide. He stared at Faith, who was concentrating on the roadway. "No, I mean the three of us. What? You don't think I see the way that you two respond to one another?"

Faith blushed, she was glad her back was to him. Damian's grin was also genuine. "Yes, she is someone special to me. I'm sure mom will love her as much as I do." The others exploded with excitement.

Faith's eyes became moist from the heartfelt words because she felt the same for him. She continued driving as she struggled to keep her emotions in check.

52.

Lieutenant Satchel was taken by surprise at the turn of events, his mind desperately tried to piece together what was going on. *How could this be happening when everything is going so well? Where could the leak be coming from?* He sat in a holding area located in the sub-level of the defense building.

Two military police officers appeared at the door. The lieutenant was escorted to a conference room filled with high ranking staff members in uniforms. A stenographer sat to the side taking notes. Lieutenant Satchel entered the room observing the executive heads from each branch of the armed forces. He felt elated. *They've come to my rescue. Now maybe I can explain this mishap.* A slight smile formed on his lips.

The meeting was now in session. The preliminary meeting was a formal action before the congressional interrogation was to began.

The line of questioning quickly took an unexpected turn. Lieutenant Satchel realized he was being used as a scapegoat.

General Major Weatherby spoke into a microphone stationed at his table. "Lieutenant Satchel, the President of the United States has ordered this inquiry. Documents obtained informed us about shipments of a prohibited chemical called thandiasine has turned up at port with billing from your department. Your signature is on the documents." The documents were passed to Lieutenant Satchel for inspection. "That is your signature, am I right? Remember, you are under oath."

"Y-yes, that is my signature. What's going on?"

"Please, just answer the questions." The questioning continued.

With each inquiry, Lieutenant Satchel felt betrayed by the group. He realized it was survival of the fittest and somehow the information leak led to him; he was the fall guy. *If you think this is the end of me, you're gravely mistaken. You've just opened the gates of hell.* Lieutenant Satchel sat fuming with anger. "I will not answer anymore questions without my lawyer present."

"Very well." Lieutenant Satchel was escorted back to his quarters.

Lieutenant Satchel paced back and forth in the holding area. The confined enclosure was nothing more than an office area no longer in service. The room held remnants of dated office furniture. The walls were stripped bare, sheet rock paneling and metal stud framing were exposed. The area was under renovation. The roof was also under repair. Ceiling panels were missing. Wires and ventilation ducts were visible. An idea occurred; the lieutenant stopped pacing. He sat on a dated leather sofa unmindful of the plaster shavings that littered the seat. His mind was preoccupied with other thoughts. *So this is what it has come to? Throw me under the bus because you can't keep your mouths shut? I'll show you.* His mind was in overdrive with anger, he fought desperately to suppress the emotion. His military training taught him emotions could cloud his judgement.

***

The conversion van driven by Faith drove onto a visitor parking area. The media was out in full force near the White House. The subject was about the chaos that hit the country in the past few days. The American people wanted answers.

"It's probably related to the violent outburst happening across the entire country," said Genesis.

"I have an idea," exclaimed Dr Baden. He rushed toward the media. The group remained close behind. As soon as Dr Baden approached, mobile news crews thrust microphones in front of his face.

"Who are you? What do you have to add to this strange phenomenon we are all experiencing across the country?" asked the announcer.

"My name is Dr Baden. I have proof the defense department is behind what is going on in the country. With me are six people that were infected. The good news is I was able to cure them."

The camera panned the group. "Are you insinuating there's a cure and nothing is being done about it?"

"What I'm saying is that our lives are in danger for what we now know. The media is the only safeguard we have if we are to stay alive. This is a massive ongoing conspiracy."

More camera crews and media officials converged on the scene. Media staff jockeyed for position to get an interview with Dr Baden and the others. The scene became a frenzy with pushing and shoving. Cellphones were used to conveyed the breaking news to other affiliate organizations across the country and globe.

53.

"Can you believed what's happening detective?"asked Detective Walters. They left the crime scene where the body of the chief editor was found murdered.

"No I cannot. Mr Lexmark's body was tortured by a professional. Maybe the forensic team will discover clues."

"I hope you're right. Let's go see what's going on with your girls." They entered an unmarked vehicle and drove away.

The detectives entered the gruesome scene involving Zesty and Cheryl. The detention center was saturated with law enforcement officials. They entered the detention center and was escorted to the crime scene by a correction officer. Detective Byrd became distraught as he viewed the scene. Self-guilt for the deaths of the women consumed him. *I should have handled the case better. I will never get them the justice they deserve.*

Detective Walters noticed the discomfort his friend displayed. He patted him on the shoulder. "You alright?"

"Yeah sure, it's just this doesn't make any kind of sense. Somehow I feel responsible."

"I'll tell you what we can do. We can make sure they didn't die in vain. Let's get to Washington and use the information we have. Maybe we can rattle some trees over there."

The plane smoothly descended on the tarmac at the Baltimore-Maryland-Washington Airport. A rental vehicle was reserved. Detective Byrd commandeered the vehicle through the busy streets of Washington, DC.

"After we make our claim, then what?" asked Detective Byrd. He kept his eyes on the roadway.

"I say we…" A breaking news report sounded on the radio. The two men listened attentively. Neither believed what was being broadcasted. "Can you believe what is going on?"

"If I didn't hear it with my own ears, I wouldn't have believe it." Detective Byrd listened to the comments spoken by Dr Baden on the radio. The detectives studied one another's expression for a moment. Detective Byrd applied pressure on the accelerator, the vehicle responded by gaining momentum. "We're a few blocks away."

***

Dr Baden recited the accounts from his research. Two military police officers approached the group from behind. A huge crowd gathered. Media cameras continuously filmed the exchange.

"Excuse me Dr Baden, your presence is requested inside," stated a military officer.

Dr Baden faced the guard. "Only if the press can attend."

"I'm sorry, but that is against regulations."

"Then I cannot accommodate you." The doctor shook his head in full view of the cameras.

The officer's voice became stern. "Sir, you must have misunderstood. This is a direct order."

"A direct order? From who? I'm a civilian, a civil servant of the people. I'm not affiliated with any military branch."

The military police officer grasped Dr Baden by the arm in efforts to detain him. The crowd became furious toward the aggression of the officer. The masses were agitated after learning how the government used citizens as test subjects without consent. The officer tried to detain the doctor, but the crowd responded by rushing to his aid. Stan, Genesis, Dexter, Rufus, and Damian followed suit. The officer was wrestled to the ground while another officer met the same fate. The entire scene was caught on film and sent across the country by way of social media. The scene took on a chaotic dimension. The setting resemble a Black Lives Matter protest where the government overstepped its boundaries once again.

***

"Look! Over there!" shouted Detective Walters. Noise crescendoed as they neared. Protesters chanted as the atmosphere became emotionally charged. The detectives rushed through the crowd with their badges on display. Other military police appeared on the scene in efforts to regain control. Detective Walters and Detective Byrd made their way to the forefront. Dr Baden and Detective Walters' eyes met, neither expected the outcome. The detective felt the case was coming to a full circle.

"Dr Baden don't worry, you'll not have to go with them. You are under my jurisdiction," said Detective Walters.

The military police parted the crowd for a man wearing an ash-gray two-piece suit. He was obviously a man of distinction by the way the soldiers saluted him and cleared an opening for his approach. He wore a white shirt, black tie, and black wing-tip shoes. His clean shaven face and sky-blue eyes contrasted greatly with the dark fabric of his suit. He approached Dr Baden.

"Excuse me Dr Baden. I'm Deputy Director Carl Ramses. I'm from the Department of Defense. I am sorry for the mishap in communication here. We are investigating this outbreak in the country and we haven't found any solution as of yet. Your hypothesis is very intriguing and would like for you to share your enlightenment with the committee."

"On one account…" Dr Baden glanced at the two detectives. He also gazed at the others. "I want my group permitted to join in."

Deputy Director Carl Ramses studied the gathering crowd and noticed cameras trained on him. He realized the news feeds were live and broadcasted all across the country. "I don't see why not."

"Very well then." They were escorted toward a fenced enclosure. It was guarded by armed soldiers. The media remained at the front entrance for an initial follow up on the subject.

54.

Lieutenant Satchel had no intentions of waiting around for dessert to be served. He hoisted himself atop a dusty desk and made his way into an air duct. The ventilation passageway provided fresh air into the complex. The lieutenant realized the duct meant an outside source to freedom. He snaked his way through the dark and dusty labyrinth of passageways. Although dressed in uniform, he had no time to consider his appearance. He was fueled by revenge, his mind was focused on fleeing from captivity. Time passed, Lieutenant Satchel exited the shaft at an industrial section of the compound. Large generators hummed in the background. Heavy machinery and skids of construction supplies were placed around the area. He took in a deep inhalation of fresh air. Noticing the sun directly overhead, he figured the time to be around noonish. The lieutenant dusted off his uniform with his hands and headed toward the east gate. He returned a salute to an officer manned at the gate and continued onward. The lieutenant's mind was systematically on his next engagement. He stopped at a general store to purchase a prepaid cellphone. For what he had in mind, he didn't want to leave a paper trail. After the purchase, he flagged a taxicab and headed toward the airport. By the time the authorities cordoned off the area he would be at his destination. Before exiting the taxicab he made a call and gave specific instructions to the receiver of the call. The taxicab stopped in front of the Baltimore-Maryland-Washington Airport.

***

Dr Baden, Genesis, Damian, Faith, and the rest of the group were led to a large conference room where staff moved about working. A stenographer sat off to the side. Four uniformed men, each represented a different branch of the armed forces, were seated around a huge table. Deputy Director Carl Ramses sat off to the side as an observant. The distinguished men sat around a large rectangular table. Detective Walters and Detective Byrd sat with the group.

"Okay, the observatory investigation will began," stated the deputy director. "Why don't you go first Dr Baden. The others can go systematically afterward."

Dr Baden stated his name and position and began revealing his findings. He started with his encounter with Genesis at the hospital, and exposed his findings with the tattoo parlors, and the illegal access of thandiasine. He explained the medical side effects of the chemical in each person. When he was finish, the next person approached the podium to explain their dilemma. At the conclusion of testimonies, the four uniformed executives gazed at one another knowingly. The deputy director spoke.

"Okay, we've heard everyone's account of the situation. We will consider each account as we investigate further. The only one left to call upon is Lieutenant Satchel who is being detained on the premises." He motioned for the military police officer to escort the lieutenant to the chamber.

Two military police officers walked down a corridor in the sub-level of the complex. They approached a guard who stood watch near a steel door. The enclosure housed Lieutenant Satchel.

"We have orders to escort the lieutenant to the committee room," stated the arriving officer.

The officer standing guard used his key to gain access. The three entered the quarters and glanced around the unoccupied room. Expressions of bewilderment were displayed on each man's face.

"Check the bathroom," ordered the officer.

The responding officer knocked on the door. "Lieutenant Satchel will you please come out of the bathroom!" Not receiving a response, he forcefully gained entrance. The room was empty. "He's not here! Call the commanding officer and notify the gates."

The meeting in the chamber was still underway. A military officer entered. He approached the deputy director and whispered into his ear. Others noticed the interruption as the officer stepped back, saluted the director, and exited the room. The director stood facing the group.

"I'm sorry, we'll have to adjourn this meeting until further notice. You are excused. Everything will be investigated. If needed you will be notified."

The group was dismayed at the sudden discontinuance. Detective Walters and Detective Byrd sensed something of importance had just taken place. They all headed out of the chamber.

The group were met by an aggressive media personnel. The crews rushed forward to get an exclusive interview. Dr Baden felt he owed them that much and stepped into the den of microphones and cameras. Flashbulbs illuminated continuously. The group remained in the background close to the the doctor.

"So detective…" Genesis related to Detective Walters. She spoke in a whispery tone. "Are we still under arrest after all you've witnessed?"

Detective Walters smiled. As a matter of fact no. You're not being detained. Remember, make yourself available if I need you." He gave her a knowingly wink.

***

AREA 5 is a parking area used for high-ranking employees and diplomates. The location is secure with two armed guards posted in a booth at the front entrance. A military vehicle approached the gate and stopped. A guard approached the vehicle and was handed a document by the driver.

"I'm here to pick up an attaché, a Mr Theodore Dreiser. He's an ambassador at the American Embassy. I'm to drive him to the United Nations building. I'm also told there might be a delay in his appearance."

The guard studied the document and glanced into the interior of the vehicle from where he stood. "One moment please." He headed toward the shack to confirm the paperwork.

The driver sat calmly, his fingers tapped gently on the top of the dashboard. He knew the document would stand up to any scrutiny. The guard returned and handed the document to the driver. The driver was also dressed in a service uniform.

"Everything checks out, you can park over there. They said it may be a twenty five minute wait."

"Yes sir." The vehicle moved toward the rear of the area and parked in a position that allowed only the driver side to be viewed from the booth where the two guards were stationed. The engine was shut off. The driver waited in his vehicle as the two guards at the booth were busy checking credentials of motorists and didn't pay him any attention.

"Okay now!" He whispered toward the rear compartment of the vehicle. A rustling sound emitted. Behind the driver's seat was another soldier. He was crouched in a low position. Tarp covered him from view. He sprung into action when he heard the command.

The soldier wore military fatigues. He began moving methodically in the back of the vehicle. He gathered the gear needed and eased open the rear door. The soldier was out of view from the guard post. His short and slim physic was perfect for the clandestine operation underway. Continuing to crouch, he made his way toward a civilian vehicle. The soldier rolled underneath and began carrying out his orders. Five minutes later, he rolled from that vehicle to another.

Repeating the same procedure, he finished two more vehicles. The total amount of vehicles he serviced were four. Within minutes he was back in the vehicle in which he arrived. He repositioned himself in obscurity and waited.

The driver of the vehicle smiled as he checked his watch. He started the engine and slowly approached the gates. A guard appeared from the booth.

"They just called in a last minute cancellation. I wish those suits would make up their minds," stated the driver.

The guard smiled. "Amen to that. Have a good drive back to the base."

"Will do." The vehicle moved forward toward the main roadway.

55.

"How could this have happened?" General Major Weatherby was irate.

A military officer stood at attention outside the quarters where Lieutenant Satchel was once detained. "Sir we have no knowledge. We were ordered to stand watch in front of the entrance. Our orders were not to allow any admittance or exit. With all due respect, we carried that order out sir."

General Major Weatherby knew what the officer said was true. The information did not eliminate the frustration that amounted within. A great deal of the department's budget was spent on cultivating the new weapon. *How could this go so wrong?*

General Carson was also concerned. He walked around the small enclosure looking for clues. "He couldn't have just vanished. Hell, if I knew he had that ability, we could have used him in another capacity.

He walked near a wall at the rear of the room, his attention was captured by an out of place substance. General Carson stooped to pick up a few pieces of foreign matter and studied it closely.

"What have you got there Joe?" asked General Major Weatherby curiously.

The general analyzed the substance for a moment. "It looks like…" He glanced up at the ceiling. A smile ensued. "That's how the bastard did it!" he exclaimed. He pointed his finger toward the ventilation duct. "Get me the blueprints to the ventilation duct and find out where it leads. Make sure I'm kept posted." His commands were to the military police present.

"The deputy director is going to make a lot of trouble for us. I suggest we get out of here and prepare our statements together. That way it will all coincide with the lieutenant's demise," remarked General Major Weatherby.

As dawn approached, the evening sky darkened to a bluish-gray hue. Four executive officers exited the building onto the secured parking area called Area 5.

Each man headed toward their vehicle and entered. Their engines started almost simultaneously. Each officer was preoccupied in thoughts. There was a preordained location for just the kind of situation they found themselves entangled in. The contingency plan was to get to a safe location to discuss the new details privately.

Approximately two minutes after each engine was activated, loud thunderous explosions erupted. The impact rocked the entire foundation of Area 5. A total of four explosions erupted successively. Metal and glass were forcefully ejected in all directions. The two guards were killed instantly when the hood of a vehicle pierced through the glass enclosure at an alarming rate of speed. Shrapnel decapitated one of the officers. The other was impaled by metal and glass; a major artery was severed killing him instantly. Black smoke and fire billowed up in the evening sky. Area 5 resembled a war zone. General Major Weatherby was the last to start his engine. For a split second he tried to react. As he witnessed the other vehicles detonate, he quickly unfastened his safety belt in an attempt to exit his vehicle. He cleared the vehicle and raced forward in efforts to find shelter as adrenaline propelled his elderly body. The distance General Major Weatherby cleared was two feet before his vehicle exploded. A powerful blast caused metal and glass to expel forcefully in all directions. A door hit him, the majority of his bones were shattered upon impact. An airborne engine from another vehicle toppled onto him sealing his fate.

***

After hearing reports and finding his name as a prime suspect, Lieutenant Satchel realized he needed extra insurance if he was to survive the ordeal. He made his way to Detroit, Michigan. During the trip he obtained information into who caused the intelligence leaks. *Dr Baden, you and your group want to interfere in my business?* Within minutes he was able to get a lead on a few of the group's whereabouts.

56.

The group watched the departure marquee inside the airport terminal. The electronic display noted flights arrivals and departures. Living in different parts of the country meant separate flights would have to be made. It was truly an emotional time for everyone. Although their encounter was brief, the time spent together was intense. The experience produced a cemented bond. Teary eyes and emotional embraces took precedence over the moment. An announcement blared over the public address system. Notification to Flight 417 to New York was now being boarded. The group divided into separate groups. Dr Baden, Faith, Genesis, and Detective Walters were in one section. Detective Byrd, Kenny, Stan, Dexter, Rufus, Chuck, and Damian took to the other side.

Dr Baden and the group headed toward the departure ramp. Detective Byrd and the others continuously waved goodbyes. Kenny gazed at Damian; silence was initiated between the two. Their eyes expressed the emotion. Kenny knew the gaze all too well, he experienced it when he met Clair. He nodded his approval to Damian.

"Go get your girl."

Damian smiled and darted through the crowd and spotted her. "Faith!" He rushed to close the gap.

Faith felt sullen because going home to an empty house was not rewarding. She wanted to remain with the guys; they made her feel wanted and needed. She stopped after hearing her name called and turned toward the sound. Faith initially thought her mind was playing a trick. Seeing him hurrying made her heart skip a beat with joy. Genesis was just as delighted and signaled to Faith with a hand gesture, and a nod of approval. The two connected at the midpoint and embraced. Facing, they gazed into one another's dreamy eyes.

"Faith, I want you to come back with me to meet my mother. I will personally take you home. What do you say?"

Through tear-soaked eyes, she nodded her approval. "Yes, I would love to meet your parents." Faith glanced at Genesis who seemingly knew all along what was taking place. Genesis and Dr Baden waived goodbyes. The two walked back toward the others hand in hand. Damian and Faith were greeted with embraces and high-fives. Kenny was genuinely happy.

"How about we go pick up the vehicle and make it home from there?"

"Sounds like a plan to me," responded Damian. The others were in agreement.

"Good, I'll call Clair and let her know we're on our way."

57.

The telephone call relieved Clair tremendously from doubtfulness. Although the news reports on television increased her apprehension level, she kept busy cooking and getting the house in a festive decorum. A caterer arrived delivering wonderful dishes. The kitchen table took on a banquet setting. A local gift shop sent over a couple of guys to help with hanging banners. Clair inspected the room and took in the ambiance after all was completed. She decided to change and wait for Kenny and Damian's arrival. She was thrilled with the news of a having a guest arrived with them. *I like surprises.*

Clair felt comfortable wearing an aqua-blue sundress with paisley design. She hurried downstairs after a knock came to the door. *They must have forgotten to use their keys in all the confusion.* Clair opened the door in anticipation of her family, but the joyous emotion faded when she eyed a man dressed in uniform standing on her porch. Clair remembered the news reported about government corruption. *Maybe he's come to tell me something about Kenny and Damian.* She stared at the man. "May I help you?"

Lieutenant Satchel faced Clair with a calmly approach and an outstretched hand. "My name is Lieutenant Satchel." He scanned the interior as he spoke. Accessing details was a strong trait he naturally possessed, he read the writing on the banner as he addressed Clair. "I am here for Kenny and Damian."

"What is this about? Is something wrong?" Clair felt sudden apprehension.

"No Mrs…"

"Washington. Kenny is my husband and Damian is my son."

"Yes of course. I see a striking resemblance. I'm here to debrief them on their early events. May I come in?"

Clair glanced at the modestly decorated uniform. *He must be someone important.* She sighed. "Sure, come in. As you can see, I was in preparation of their return. Can I get you something to drink or eat?"

"Yes, anything cold to drink would be nice. Have you spoken to them lately?"

"Why yes, they're on the way here as we speak. I'll get you something to drink. Make yourself comfortable."

Clair busied herself in the kitchen with a news radio station playing. She poured ice tea into two frosted glasses, and added lemon sections to the rims. A special news report aired; a newscaster announced the latest update concerning the spikes in violence across the country. She raised the volume slightly.

…with all the acts of aggression across the nation. In related matters, during an

observational hearing in the capitol city, Lieutenant Satchel, a prime suspect in a government scandal has escaped from a military holding facility. His whereabouts at the moment are unknown. He is now being sought. We will keep you updated on the events as they unfold. This is Sandra Battle with WTWX Channel 7...
Apprehension showered Clair emotions as she turned off the radio. She picked up the tray of drinks and turned toward the door. The tray released from her grasp.

CRASH!

Liquid and glass splattered and shattered at her feet. Clair's eyes came in direct contact with Lieutenant Satchel as he stood inches away. He heard the news report when she raised the volume.

"I wish you hadn't heard that." He shook his head dramatically.

A frightening chill overwhelmed her. "W-what do you want?"

Lieutenant Satchel's eyes displayed a faraway gaze. "I wanted a peaceful resolution, I was even prepared to be civil. I figured to have a few drinks and wait until your family members return. Then, kill you all!" He sighed deeply. "Now, I'll have to find another alternative."

Clair dashed toward a counter and picked up a butcher knife. She pointed the sharp blade toward the lieutenant. "I don't know what you're doing here, but you better leave. I don't want any trouble."

"It doesn't have to be like this." He inched toward Clair.

"Don't you come any closer! I'll use it if I have to!" Her mind worked frantically, she needed a way to alert the authorities for help.

Lieutenant Satchel noticed her hands trembled as she held onto the knife. "I'll tell you what. Why don't we just go into the living room, I'll keep my distance, and wait until the others come home as planned."

"What do you want from them?"

"That my dear is government business."

"Cut the horse shit! You're a wanted man by your own people."

Lieutenant Satchel applauded. "How smart you are." His expression was that of seriousness. "Okay, the politeness is over. Put the knife down and go sit in the living room." His voice was stern and chastising.

"You must be…" Clair poised the knife with more confidence. Although afraid, she wouldn't allow the emotion total control.

Lieutenant Satchel lunged toward the knife. Clair thrusted downward, the countermeasure enabled her to slice him across the right wrist.

"Ahh!" Lieutenant Satchel was surprised at her response. He glanced at the superficial gash on his wrist.

Clair was obviously petrified; her body trembled from fear. The weapon in her hand was unsteady as her eyes scanned the room for an escape.

"You shouldn't have done that." The lieutenant removed his uniform jacket and held it with both hands by the sleeves. The act resembled a matador enticing a bull with a cape. He charged toward his adversary.

Clair took in a deep inhalation and thrusted the blade forward. Lieutenant Satchel anticipated the move by entangling the weapon into the jacket. Pulling downward, he caused her to lose balance and release the weapon. Clair scrambled for the weapon as it slide across the floor. Suddenly, excruciating pain was felt at the back of her neck followed by unconsciousness.

Lieutenant Satchel could have easily killed Clair. He carried her limp body to a bedroom upstairs where she was tied and gagged. The lieutenant returned downstairs and waited for the return of Kenny and Damian. He chuckled as he read the banner.

58.

The trip across country was uneventful, with no mishaps. The first destination was to drop off Stan, Dexter, Chuck, and Rufus. The parents of the boys were at the doorsteps anxiously waiting to reunite with their siblings. Praises were given to Kenny for bringing them home safely. Detective Byrd was dropped off at his precinct.

"You guys be careful and mindful until they catch the lieutenant. If you have any problems make sure you give me a call." Detective Byrd handed each of them a business card.

Kenny drove to the house. Damian glanced at his mother's vehicle in the driveway.

"You're going to love mother," said Damian. He held onto Faith's hand.

Kenny peered through the window to see welcoming decorations.

He turned toward the others and whispered. "Looks like Clair went through a lot of trouble on our account. Let's act surprised." Kenny placed his key in the lock cylinder and opened the door. He anticipated the foyer light to be on; they were off. *That's odd, Clair always leaves the foyer light on. Maybe the bulb is blown.* The darkness impaired his vision as he searched for the switch and turned on the lights. Kenny was impressed with decorations. He anticipated people to appear from hiding to surprise them, that never happened. They were perplexed at the quietness. Everyone gazed around the room. There were no signs of disturbance.

"Maybe she's upstairs dressing and we've arrived too early. I'll go up and check it out. You guys make yourself comfortable," said Kenny. He checked the bathroom for Clair, it was unoccupied. Kenny turned the master bedroom door knob slowly and opened the door. His eyes widen in disbelief at the sight. Clair was on the bed bound and gagged. The scene infuriated him as he hurried to her aid. Unexpected pain engulfed the back of his neck; the force rendered him unconscious.

Lieutenant Satchel watched as the vehicle approached the house. He anticipated his next move knowing the element of surprise was on his side. The lieutenant figured he would work from higher ground instead of on the main floor. He was aware too many things could go wrong. He heard when Kenny approached the bedroom and hid behind the door. Kenny was hit with the butt of a snub-nose revolver as he entered the room. The impact was felt at the back of the neck rendering him unconscious. The lieutenant closed the door and bound Kenny's legs and hands. He left the body on the floor near the bed and waited patiently.

Damian and Faith were becoming acquainted on the main floor. Music played as they sat close to one another on a sofa.

"This is a nice place you live in. Have you lived here long?"

"Yeah, I grew up here. My biological father left this house to me and my mother. My room is in the basement. You wanna see it?"

Faith looked at him shyly, a grin was plastered on her face. "Sure," she agreed. "I'm thirsty, can you get me something to drink?"

"Okay, let's go into the kitchen. We can take our drinks downstairs. I want to show you my music collection."

The two stopped at the threshold of the kitchen. They were taken aback at the disarray. Overturned chairs, broken glass, and liquid were scattered about. Damian became alarmed.

"Momma!" Damian saw that Faith was frightened. "Stay here until I find out what is going on."

"Be careful."

Damian rushed up the stairs to check on Kenny and Clair. The wooden steps creaked as he applied his weight. "Kenny? Clair?" He he reached the upper landing. The floor layout consisted of a corridor with aligning walnut stained doors along the walls. Two of the doors were bedrooms; two were closets. The last one was a bathroom. Not receiving a response to his call, Damian reached the bedroom door and placed his ears to the smooth wood surface. He heard rustling from behind the door. He intended to barge. Suddenly, the doorknob was snatched from his grasp as the door opened inwardly. The element of surprise was in the intruder's favor. He grabbed Damian by the throat and held a death grip. The choke hold was unbreakable.

Damian couldn't believe his eyes. Clair was on the bed unmoving and Kenny on the floor. The sight caused a surge of rage to emerge. With all of his might, Damian fought to reverse the grip on this throat. He twisted and pushed. The powerful force tossed both men around the room. A lamp was the first to fall. It made a loud shattering sound as it crashed to the floor. The contents on the dresser were scattered about. Lieutenant Satchel fought strenuously to retain his grip as he was shoved against a dresser. The sound of shattering mirror was pronounced. Audible grunts were pronounce. Damian's energy was almost depleted; he felt his air supply slowly ebb from his body. Lightheadedness overwhelmed him. He was weakened by the lack of oxygen to the brain.

Faith forcefully entered the room amongst the chaos. "What is…" The lieutenant and her eyes locked. Damian's shout broke her spell.

"Faith! Run!" Damian tried to finish his sentence as he succumbed to oxygen deprivation.

Faith reversed her footing and darted out of the room. Scared, confused, and not knowing the layout of the house made matters worst. The sounds of feet pattered on the wooden stairs as she made her way to the main floor. Faith intended to head outside. She heard harsh noise behind her as she fled; the sound grew as it neared. Faith continued toward the basement in search for shelter. Her eyes darted around the room. A pool table was in the center of the room. An entertainment center and a large flatscreen television were on the right. Three doors were on the left. An open bedroom door was at the rear. Similar to choosing a door on a game show, Faith chose door number three. Inside was crowded with clothing on hangers. Some garments were in plastic bags. Faith appreciated the mess. She hid under a mound of clothes. She remain quiet and still listening for the stranger's whereabouts. Her heart beat felt as if it could be heard from the other side of the room.

Lieutenant Satchel placed Damian's unconscious body next to Kenny. He knew he could have easily killed the two. His training was superior. All he wanted at the moment was information. After restraining Damian, the lieutenant went to search for the female. He didn't hear the front door open and realized she was likely in the house. *So you wanna play hide-n-seek?* He headed out of the bedroom.

An idea came to Faith, she reached for her cellphone and dialed Detective Byrd's number. The device emitted an indigo color light; it pierced through the darkness in the small enclosure. A voice answered. Faith took in a deep inhalation to slow her breathing. She exhaled and spoke slowly; her voice held a whispery tone. "This is Faith, we're in trouble." She listened attentively all the while keeping alert for the intruder. "I don't know where I am. I'm hiding in a basement closet. I think the rest are dead." She listen to the response. Faith placed the cellphone in a black plastic bag to distinguish the light to remain connected to the call. The signal was being triangulated to reveal her location. Faith heard footsteps from above. She was frightened beyond belief; never had she experience anything so horrendous.

59.

Detective Byrd rushed from home after receiving the distressful call from Faith. Dressed in jeans, sweatshirt, and sneakers he hurried to find her. He knew with Lieutenant Satchel in the mix, their lives were in grave danger. The detective was aware the lieutenant was a trained killer for the United States. Detective Byrd drove, using his vehicle as a command center. He spoke with the precinct dispatcher. "I want you to find any information on Kenny Washington, it won't be a criminal record. Try dmv, the license plate to his vehicle will be an indicator. Triangulate this call. I'm sending you the signal now." He continued driving onward. Frustration mount because he didn't know where to begin his search for Faith. Squelch noise from a two-way radio diverted his thoughts. The dispatcher's voice filled the vehicle.

Detective Byrd. One-zero-one-eight Latimore Drive." Static followed the transmission. "I am on my way. Please send backup." Detective Byrd pressed hard on the accelerator. A thought occurred to notify Detective Walters. *What's the sense? He's too far away to be of any help.*

***

CRASH!

The sound of breakage reverberated from the other side of the door. Stricken with fear, Faith remained hidden in the closet under a pile of clothes. Pangs of loneliness and fear entered her being as she thought of Damian. A cynical voice of a crazed person resonated on the other side of the door.

"I've thoroughly searched this entire house. Do you know what that means? It means you must be in here somewhere." He gave off a crude chuckle. "Let me check over here." Lieutenant Satchel spoke in a child-like jovial voice.

CRASH!

More breakage erupted. Faith's mind worked frantically to find an escape. Another sound permeated the room. Thunderous thwacks reverberated. A door was forcefully opened. She figured he was at the first door. Her choosing door number three only prolonged the inevitable. Faith felt a hard substance at the back of her head as she laid horizontally.

Lieutenant Satchel thoroughly searched the first closet. "I'll tell you what. Come out now and I'll make it easy on you. I know you didn't have anything to do with this mess. You just gotten involved on a humbug." His laugh was sadistic. The merriment subsided immediately as the lieutenant's demented demeanor returned.

Desperation envelope Faith, she used the cellphone light to search the interior for something to protect herself. The object she felt earlier was an aerosol can. The label read anti-perspirant spray. An idea formulated. She remembered a time she attended an outdoor reggae concert. Spectators celebrated by lighting up the night sky with torches.

CLASH!

The sound abruptly returned her from her reverie. It was closer this time. The noise came from next door. She could hear him rumbling around nearby. Faith's heart rate accelerated in anticipation of her demise.

"Last chance! One more door left." The lieutenant retrieved his weapon from his jacket pocket and approached the final door. A noise from upstairs distracted him. "Shit!"

Detective Byrd raced onto a residential block. Four marked cruisers and officers waited instructions. He displayed hand signals to the men as he hurried toward the Victorian home.

The house was simultaneously breached on both sides. Detective Byrd led a group into the house. They moved methodically in a tactical manner. Detective Byrd sent the men upstairs, he alone took to the basement. A faint voice was audible as he descended the stairs.

Lieutenant Satchel placed his hand on the doorknob and slowly turned. The door creaked as it opened. He anticipated his prize behind door number three. As the door widened, the lieutenant was met with the unexpected. A fireball was ejected from the closet. His clothing was immediately ignited, he became a human inferno. Faith was afraid to exit the closet, she looked on at the horrific scene filled with apprehension. Dreadful agony engulfed the lieutenant, he desperately tried to dowse the flames with one hand while holding the weapon in the other aimed at Faith.

Faith closed her eyes in preparation for death. Visions of her mother passed across her mind, along with racing strings of events. *So this is what it's like.*

PLOP! PLOP! PLOP!

Faith flinched with each thunderous staccato report from the weapon. She didn't feel any pain; her thought was she already died and was experiencing an out-of-body ordeal. Faith opened her eyes to see Lieutenant Satchel on the floor motionless and covered in flames. A hand appeared.

Detective Byrd fired his weapon from close range. The projectiles hit the lieutenant in the body. The detective watched his flaming body go down onto the floor as he approached the closet and gently helped Faith from captivity. He saw she was disoriented. "Are you hurt?" Faith didn't answer; shock had overtaken her body. Officers converged on the scene. The fire was distinguished from the lieutenant's body and Faith was taken to an awaiting ambulance. She was driven to a nearby hospital for observation. Kenny, Damian, and Clair were also en route to the hospital.

60.

Detective Byrd arrived at the hospital the morning of their release. He drove everyone back to Kenny and Clair's house. The detective took the liberty of having the house professionally cleaned and prepped for their arrival.

Kenny, Clair, Damian, and Faith exited the vehicle. They entered their home with a sense of skepticism. Vivid memories of the event lingered.

"WELCOME HOME!

"CONGRATULATIONS!"

The sudden eruption of cheers exploded. The greetings were loud and genuine. A large banner hung from the ceiling in the living room. The entire group's names were written with festive flair on the banner. Detective Walters, Genesis, Dr Baden, Stan, Dexter, Rufus, Damian, Faith, Kenny, Clair, and Chuck's names were visible.

Everyone embraced; the gathering was heartfelt. The group entered the kitchen to enjoy a catered feast. A large table accommodated everyone in attendance. The food was a gourmet's delight.

"Has any word with the government dealings come to light yet?" asked Dr Baden.

Detective Byrd dabbed his lips with a napkin. "There was a congressional hearing. The findings were the executive heads of staff were working beyond the frame of reform. Although they had a twisted sense of good, it was wrong to use unsuspecting Americans as test subjects. The program was dismantled. All of the Urban Ink World tattoo parlors were shut down." Loud claps from the group ensued. "Also, there is a program to help everyone effected from the experiment. Even to help erase the body art performed by them."

Damian glanced across the table at Faith. Their eyes met. The visual union created smiles of endearment. On the other side of the table, Kenny and Clair's eyes connected with each other. Their eyes focused on Damian and his new friend Faith. Clair like her immediately. Kenny stood.

"I would like to propose a toast." He waited while everyone picked up a glass. "To a new future with new friends. To everlasting love." The sound of fine crystal clang.

At the conclusion of dinner, everyone made their way to the living room for music and entertainment. Faith cornered Damian in the hall and kissed him. The gesture lingered longer than expected. The aftermath wasn't awkward as each thought it would be. They felt a natural alliance, an inevitable togetherness. "You have to come to my house to meet my mother," said Faith. She displayed a sly wink.

escapehatch100@gmail.com

www.ingramcontent.com/pod-product-compliance
Lightning Source LLC
Chambersburg PA
CBHW070219030726
47505CB00006B/1729